Love was dangerous for a McKenna.

Suddenly Ella was in his arms, and Tiernan wasn't certain if he'd pulled her there or if she'd thrown herself against him. All he knew was the rightness of the close contact. Of the certainty that this was meant to be. That he was meant to hold her. Kiss her.

And then he was.

Her lips were soft and dewy. A cry deep in her throat signaled her need, and without thinking, he responded, deepening the kiss until he tasted her soul. Mouths linked, bodies pressed together, he imagined them joined as one, unfettered by anything but pure emotion and raw desire.

He had never experienced anything quite like that with another woman. There had to be a reason for it.

Fate. Something he couldn't avoid.

Dear Reader,

Thank you for your loyalty, for keeping Harlequin Intrigue in your hearts for twenty-five years and for continuing to read my Intrigue stories since *Double Images* was published in 1986.

I have been lucky enough to write all different types of stories for the Intrigue line. I started with romantic mysteries, progressed to romantic suspense and romantic thrillers and now write mostly paranormal romantic suspense or thrillers. I've always appreciated the opportunity to stretch and exercise my creativity within the line.

Stealing Thunder is my forty-ninth Intrigue and the first in a new branch of the McKennas. I hope you enjoy it and all my Intrigue novels to follow.

Good reading,

Patricia Rosemoor

PATRICIA ROSEMOOR

STEALING THUNDER

TORONTO • NEW YORK • LONDON
AMSTERDAM • PARIS • SYDNEY • HAMBURG
STOCKHOLM • ATHENS • TOKYO • MILAN • MADRID
PRAGUE • WARSAW • BUDAPEST • AUCKLAND

Thanks to the writers who are always willing to brainstorm with me—Marc for the movie set and Sherrill, Cheryl and Rosemary for the big finish.

ISBN-13: 978-0-373-69416-7

STEALING THUNDER

This edition published by arrangement with Harlequin Books S.A.

www.eHarlequin.com

Printed in U.S.A.

ABOUT THE AUTHOR

Patricia Rosemoor has always had a fascination with dangerous love. She loves bringing a mix of thrills and chills and romance to Harlequin Intrigue readers. She's won a Golden Heart from Romance Writers of America and Reviewers' Choice and Career Achievement Awards from *Romantic Times BOOKreviews.* She teaches courses on writing popular fiction and suspense-thriller writing in the fiction writing department of Columbia College Chicago. Check out her Web site, www.PatriciaRosemoor.com. You can contact Patricia either via e-mail at Patricia@PatriciaRosemoor.com, or through the publisher at Patricia Rosemoor, c/o Harlequin/Silhouette Books, 233 Broadway, New York, NY 10279.

Books by Patricia Rosemoor

HARLEQUIN INTRIGUE

707—VIP PROTECTOR†
745—THE BOYS IN BLUE
"Zachary"
785—VELVET ROPES†
791—ON THE LIST†
858—GHOST HORSE
881—RED CARPET CHRISTMAS†
924—SLATER HOUSE
958—TRIGGERED RESPONSE
1031—WOLF MOON*
1047—IN NAME ONLY?*
1101—CHRISTMAS DELIVERY
1128—RESCUING THE VIRGIN*
1149—STEALING THUNDER

*The McKenna Legacy
†Club Undercover

CAST OF CHARACTERS

Tiernan McKenna—A horse wrangler. He wants to find justice for a victim he didn't know because of something he couldn't control in his past.

Ella Thunder—The history teacher is driven to learn the truth about her father's death.

Joseph Thunder—Why was the shaman really killed?

Harold Walks Tall—How was his death connected to Joseph's?

Marisala Saldana—What did the Lakota actress know before she lost her mind?

Nathan Lantero—The activist may have political reasons to want to shut the movie down.

Leonard Hawkins—Does the casino owner know more than he's willing to admit?

Jimmy Iron Horse—The head of tribal police seems more interested in threatening Ella than in finding a murderer.

June 22, 1919

Donal McKenna,

Ye might have found happiness with another woman, but yer progeny will pay for this betrayal of me. I call on my faerie blood and my powers as a witch to give yers only sorrow in love, for should they act on their feelings, they will put their loved ones in mortal danger.

So be it,

Sheelin O'Keefe

Prologue

Bitter Creek Reservation, South Dakota

"Come out and meet your accusers, sorcerer!"

The deep voice rumbled through the crowd. Thirteen-year-old Ella Thunder felt a cold lump in her chest as her father jerked her away from the window and the sight of angry faces surrounding the house. Half the people who lived on the rez awaited him.

"Go to your room, Ella!"

Trembling, Ella backed into the doorway of her bedroom, but she refused to go inside. She wouldn't abandon her father!

A rugged man with features as craggy as the South Dakota Badlands, Joseph Thunder radiated power as he stepped toward the front door. Ella only hoped his power was strong enough to save him.

"Joseph, no," Mother said, her delicate white hands catching on her husband's muscular bronze arm. "They're beyond reason! We should have left once the rumors started."

Ella had heard the disgusting rumors. How her shaman father was secretly doing bad things. How he'd taken Nelson Bird's mind from him because Nelson had caught him.

Lies!

"Out, sorcerer!" thundered the voice. "Before we burn down your house!"

As Father reached for the handle, Ella rushed past him and threw herself against the door. "No!" Her heart was beating as fast as a hummingbird's wings. "Let *me* go. I'll tell them they're wrong!"

"Ah, Ella. There was never a braver girl." Father's dark eyes filled with sadness, and he kissed the top of her head. "Someday you'll have great need for that bravery, to get you through a journey of terrible danger. But not this day. This day is mine alone to suffer."

She fought him, but she couldn't stop him from pulling her away from the door. A lump in her throat threatened to choke her, and her eyes burned.

Mother's blue eyes filled with tears as she pleaded, "Joseph, please *do* something. Use your power to stop them!"

The request shocked Ella and made her recognize the depth of Mother's desperation. Her mother believed in Christian teachings, not in the mystical powers of the Lakota.

"Some things are predestined and no power is strong enough to stop them."

Ella knew her father never used his power for himself, but only to help others—and wondered if that was a personal decision, or something not of his choosing, that he was bound to.

His forehead drawn into a scowl, Father stepped out onto the dirt road and spoke to the crowd. "Don't let wild talk overcome your good sense!"

Seeming as if they were struck speechless by this horror, the grandparents huddled together at the kitchen table, holding on to her younger sister, Miranda, as if waiting for the judgment call of the crowd.

Ella wasn't going to wait. She ran out into the street in

time to hear Roderick Bird, Nelson's older brother, accusing her father.

"What you did to Nelson is proof enough for me that you practice sorcery!"

"I did no evil to Nelson—"

"Liar!" came a chorus of voices.

"You've brought disease and poverty to the rez," one woman yelled, "so we have no future!"

"The future is in the earth beneath your feet," Joseph said. "You must believe—"

"Get him!"

The crowd surrounded her father and dragged him toward the church. "No!" Ella screamed, trying to reach him. "No!"

"Leave Joseph alone!" Mother yelled. "He is innocent!"

But the crowd was too frenzied to listen. Wearing a venomous expression, Ami Badeau shoved Ella out of the way, and an elbow to her chin from another woman made her see stars. She tripped over a rut in the road and fell to her knees. Dazed, she saw Mother chase the crowd.

This wasn't happening, Ella thought, her chest squeezing tight. Their neighbors…people who'd come to Father for help when they were sick or needed spiritual or practical advice… they weren't themselves. Their faces had changed, their eyes burned with madness. Only her father's apprentices Leonard Hawkins and Nathan Lantero, who was also her cousin, appeared sane.

"Let him go!" Leonard yelled.

"Stop and think what you're doing!" Nathan added.

Jimmy Iron Horse, Father's third apprentice, was part of the angry crowd. He shoved Nathan out of the way. "We know what we're doing! Getting rid of a sorcerer who is bringing his evil to the rez!"

Nathan and Leonard physically tried to get to Father, to stop the mob, but they were only two and were easily shrugged away.

It was up to her to do something! Ella thought, vaguely noting the green tinge to the sky. She scrambled to her feet, but the earth itself seemed to have shifted, and the air felt thick, as if it was trying to hold her back.

As if someone had cast a spell…

Concentrating on parting the dense air like she would a curtain, she plunged into the crowd. Voices rose into a chant, and she smelled smoke. She shoved one dancing woman out of the way and squeezed past another who was singing a death chant. Then she stumbled into the open circle where her father was already bound to a post, his hands behind him, wood stacked around his legs, the track of a raven—a long line intersected with an upside down V—drawn on his forehead in black. Father appeared stricken at her presence.

Ella locked gazes with him. *What should I do? Tell me!*

Go, Ella, get out of here!

No, I won't!

Her heart thumped with a strange beat. As men with burning torches approached, Jimmy Iron Horse among them, her head went light. The flicker of something powerful and scary blossomed inside her.

Ella let go and felt her mind opening….

The sky darkened...the clouds stretched...the earth rumbled….

"No, Ella!" Father yelled. Even hunted and bound he was aware…one with the earth as was she. "It's not time! You're not ready for this! Nathan, stop her before she is destroyed!"

Hands gripped her hard and whipped her around and the earth tilted. She looked up into a distorted face and blinked to make her cousin come into focus.

"Nathan! Help me free him!"

"We're not strong enough to stop this, Ella."

She kicked Nathan hard. His grip loosened just enough to let her pull away from him. She turned to see the kindling already burning. Flames licked her father's body. The smell of flesh and hair scorched her senses.

"Nooo!"

Ella launched herself toward him, bare hands beating at the flames, ignoring the heat shooting up one arm as her sleeve ignited. Nathan tackled her and rolled her along the ground, smothering the flames.

Father!

The word echoed over and over in her mind as Nathan covered her eyes so she couldn't watch her father burn.

Chapter One

Black Hills, South Dakota, 15 years later

A wave of homesickness as wide and deep as the Irish Sea swept through Tiernan McKenna as he sat his roan gelding Red Crow and studied the Bitter Creek Mustang Refuge—grassy meadows amidst winding rugged canyons, ragged rock spires backing pine and cedar forest.

The trees gave the Black Hills their name, because from a distance, the foliage made the mountains look black. Missing the rolling land and lush green valleys of the Emerald Isle, Tiernan gazed out over the valley below, where mustangs grazed. Nothing like the Thoroughbreds he'd worked with all his life, horses he'd trained and ridden, these horses were feral.

He'd thought this was what he wanted—a complete change from his old life, a way to get out of his brother Cashel's shadow, a chance to cowboy. He'd grown up watching old American Westerns on the telly. *Cimarron, The Magnificent Seven, High Noon, Billy the Kid*—those were only some of the movies that had entranced him. So here he was in the American West and ironically, an historical Western film called *Paha Sapa Gold* was just starting to shoot in the Black

Hills, mostly on refuge land, thereby infusing the organization with sorely needed money.

Longing seared Tiernan as he gazed out on the film's camp in the distance. There were trailers for the production staff and the stars behind the supposed Main Street, though mostly facades like cardboard cutouts represented the town. The only interior sets here were the jail and the saloon. The remaining interiors would be shot in an L.A. studio.

On adjoining reservation land backed by ragged pinnacles of rock, a dozen tepees made up the Lakota Sioux village set. And up in the hills—Tiernan wasn't certain if it was reservation land or refuge—was the sealed-off entrance to an old gold mine. He'd heard the production company was planning to use that, too, since *Paha Sapa Gold* referred to the Custer Expedition's search for gold in the Black Hills despite it being Sioux land.

In the flat below were two side-by-side fenced pastures, empty now, that would hold the horses to be ridden in the film. They would come both from the MKF Ranch where he worked and from the reservation. Even the refuge mustangs would be used as a wild herd in a couple of scenes.

Too bad he wasn't part of that—the old films had fascinated him, had enticed him to make his move from Ireland to America. Well, that and not wanting to answer to Cashel anymore. Whether it was horses to train or psychic abilities to control or women to woo, Tiernan didn't want to be second best to his older brother anymore. He needed to be his own man, wherever that would take him.

So, after considering long and hard, Tiernan had left Ireland to make a life of his own. Second cousins had taken him in, had allowed him to test himself, to see if this life really was for him. While satisfying, the reality of it—the hard, dirty, unromantic work of cowboying, the answering to yet another relative—took the luster out of those films he'd loved so much. He'd thought that, like the silver-screen cowboys, he would find a way to make his own mark, on his own terms.

Now he realized he'd been telling himself a fairy tale.

Now a confused Tiernan didn't know what he wanted.

Now, missing his brothers Cashel and Aidan despite himself, missing Ma and Da, missing the green countryside and near-daily rains that brought life to Ireland's estates separated by hedgerows and limestone fences and paved roads, he wasn't so certain.

Had he made the biggest mistake of his life in leaving behind everything he knew and loved?

McKenna pride wouldn't allow him to admit it, to go crawling back—he had to make a go of it here. He had to prove to himself that he would find that elusive something that would give him the mantle of responsibility and make him feel like his own man.

Riding out on the Bitter Creek Mustang Refuge run by his cousin Kate and her husband, Chase Brody, alone on his day off, Tiernan felt even more lost as he was swept up in a timeless, borderless land without end—nothing but raw nature in every direction, not even a road in sight. The sensations filling him were simply overwhelming.

For all he knew he could be days—weeks, months—from civilization…he could simply imagine it….

Below, the feral horses stirred, then were instantly on the move. Flight instinct kicking in, they roared down the valley as one unit—grays and chestnuts and bays and sorrels and Pintos and Paints. His own mount danced and squealed, and a wave of psychic energy that nearly obliterated his vision engulfed Tiernan as he fought to keep the gelding under control. He shook away the dark, sought the reason in the opposite direction, looking to the forested red cliffs, expecting to see a mountain lion, the only real predator to threaten the herd.

Nothing jumped out at him, neither man nor beast, but once infected with the fear, he knew something—or someone—was out there.

About to take his mount down to the valley to look for the danger, he was startled to hear his name yelled from behind.

"Tiernan, wait! I want to talk to you!"

He turned in the saddle and saw Kate Brody riding straight for him. Kate was one of his second cousins, her mother being a McKenna, and them having the same great-grandparents. Feisty and outspoken, she was a veterinarian, able to sit a horse or doctor it as well as anyone he'd met.

The smothering sensation of a moment ago flitted away like the morning mist. "A good afternoon to you," he said as Kate drew alongside him, her freckled face wreathed in a smile, her wild red hair poking out from under her brimmed hat.

"I have great news. It's Quin—he just got the call. He's going to be chief of police of Blackwood, which is only thirty-some miles north of here. Everyone's so excited!"

"How grand for him."

"For us all. That means he'll stay and not disappear again."

Tiernan was closest in age to Kate's youngest brother, Quinlan Farrell, who'd been a federal agent working mostly undercover until he'd recently returned to his home state with his wife-to-be, Luz Delgado. The Farrells were throwing a big engagement party for the couple. Quin had been hoping for a lawman's job in a smaller venue and now he had one. Well, good for him. Tiernan could appreciate a man wanting to cut his own path rather than follow the one his family set out for him. Quin was lucky his family was so supportive of his choice.

"What about the film?" Tiernan asked, suddenly thinking of the responsibility Quin had taken on. "Surely Quin can't still work on it in addition to handling a new job."

Since Chase and Kate were too busy keeping the refuge

going, they'd hired Quin to be their liaison with the production company—a temporary stopgap until he landed something more permanent. The company had barely taken up residence. Filming would begin in the next few days.

"Of course Quin can't do both jobs," Kate said. "So Chase and I were wondering if *you* would consider taking over for him."

"Me?" Even as he questioned her, his pulse quickened. "I know nothing about filmmaking."

"But you do know how to wrangle horses. That and acting as a buffer when the crew needs something from us is basically all you need to do."

Somehow Tiernan didn't think the job would be quite so simple, but he didn't care. This opportunity seemed heaven-sent.

"What about your parents?" Tiernan had been working on the MKF Ranch since arriving from Ireland. "They will be counting on me—"

"Already taken care of," Kate assured him.

His enthusiasm for coming to South Dakota renewed, he said, "I'm your man, then."

"Good. I need to check on the volunteers—they're out mending fences. We'll talk more this evening. Dinner at our place. You can move in with us. We have a spare bedroom and bath. Pack your things and bring them over about six."

With that, Kate turned her mare and moved off.

And a smiling Tiernan turned back toward the red cliffs where he'd sensed the threat that had panicked the herd and decided to investigate.

WHY COULDN'T SHE be happy? Ella Thunder wondered. Having just driven in from Sioux Falls, she'd turned off the highway and had cut across land that was now a mustang refuge, a shortcut to the rez. Halfway there, she'd stopped in the shelter of some pines and gotten out of her SUV to get a better look at the herd and to reconnect with the land. Something had spooked the mustangs, though. They'd raced across the valley as if death was nipping at their hooves.

The thought reminded her of the reason Mother had taken her and Miranda to her own people and kept her daughters away from the rez to keep them safe. Fifteen years and Ella was finally returning for a short visit, all because of a film. All despite Mother's objections. A high school history teacher, Ella had written a textbook on Native American peoples in South Dakota for her students. After reading Ella's book for research, Jane Grant, the producer of *Paha Sapa Gold*, had hired her as a consultant.

Ella had gone through the screenplay and made several suggestions to make the story more authentic. Because Jane thought Ella's perspective might be useful when filming the spiritual tribal scenes, she'd hired Ella to come on set at least for a few weeks.

A job that would make Ella face her past.

It was time.

She didn't want to live as she'd been doing anymore…no more than a shadow in this world. Part of her had died with Father in that nightmare she'd tucked to the far reaches of her mind. She didn't stray there anymore, not on purpose, but sometimes her mind betrayed her and she had no choice but to relive the unthinkable.

Ella fought it, then unable to help herself, closed her eyes and saw Father tied to the stake. The air around her stirred as it always did with his presence.

It's time, he tells her as the fire licks at his feet.

Time for what? Ella asks.

The journey…

Journey? Father, what do you mean?

Danger everywhere, he says. *Look to your other half, for only then will you be whole.*

As quickly as her father had entered her mind, he was gone.

Ella opened her eyes and the earth came back into focus. She rubbed her left arm, the scarred area a little stiff from the long drive in air-conditioning.

That wasn't a memory. Then what had it been?

Nothing like this—Father talking to her as if he were still alive—had ever happened to her before. What did Father mean by *her other half?*

Her chest tightened and her stomach knotted. That fateful day, Father had said she wasn't ready, that she would be destroyed…but now he was saying it was time? Or was *she* telling herself this, conjuring her father herself? Fear licked at invisible wounds, and Ella huddled within herself at the enormity of the charge.

"Oh, Father, I don't know."

But part of her did. Some intuitive part deep in her soul. Father had said she would need her bravery for a journey of terrible danger. She'd remembered that when she'd accepted the consultant job on *Paha Sapa Gold.* When she'd gone against her mother's wishes and agreed to return to the place of nightmares.

Ella closed her eyes and tried to call her father back so that he could explain further, so that he could tell her what he expected her to do.

Father, I need you….

But the air around her remained still.

When nothing further happened, Ella decided to get going. The grandparents would be waiting, her return a momentous event in their quiet lives. Mother had insisted her returning to the rez would be a huge mistake, but Ella didn't regret coming to reconnect with the grandparents who wanted to know her in person again. Grandparents she hadn't seen in fifteen years.

Despite her arthritic hands, Grandmother was too stubborn to give in to the affliction. Ella knew this from their phone conversations, even as she knew Grandmother would have been cooking since dawn, to celebrate the return of her granddaughter.

Was there true reason to celebrate?

Though Ella was no less determined to return to the rez, doubt had set in after signing the contract with the movie company. Was she really ready to face her past and the people responsible for her father's death? Who had started the rumors? Who had whipped the crowd into a feeding frenzy? Would she know them when she saw them?

Picking her way back to her SUV, she heard a twig snap nearby and froze. Her pulse fluttered. Focusing in on the sounds around her, she heard an explosive squeak like that made by the tail feathers of a hummingbird…in the opposite direction, the low, throaty noise of a jackrabbit in distress…and directly behind her a whispered footfall that reminded her of a cougar preparing to pounce.

That would account for the mustang herd taking off, she thought, scanning the ground wildly for a weapon and spotting a softball-sized rock.

Before she could reach for it, a sharp pain in the back of her head accompanied by an explosion of light confused her senses, made everything go in and out of focus, sent her reeling, facedown into the earth.

FOR ALL HIS curiosity, Tiernan hadn't expected to find anything, so when he spotted the dark green SUV sheltered under a boxelder amidst the pines, he stiffened, his surprise touching Red Crow, who danced sideways. Not making a sound, Tiernan held the gelding in check and focused all six senses.

What came to him strongest was a blinding pain. He let go and the pain subsided and his vision cleared.

Dismounting, he looped the horse's reins in a low branch of a pine and moved carefully to the left, through a scattering of trees, toward a clearing overlooking the meadow valley. That's when he saw her—an attractive lass in jeans and a long-sleeved cotton shirt, dark hair flowing down her back in a thick ponytail. She was sitting on the ground, trying to get to her feet but not quite managing.

Tiernan rushed to her side to help, but what he got for his trouble when he touched her arm and murmured, "Easy, there," was a fist square in his chest.

The air rushed out of him and he let go of her and she scrabbled back, staring at him with wide-open amber eyes. "Get away from me, or I'll…I'll…"

She looked around wildly—for a weapon, he supposed.

"You'll what?" he asked in the soft, melodic voice he used when working with horses, a voice meant to calm and seduce. "I'll not be hurting you."

"You knocked me out!"

"'Tis someone else you need to be accusing. I just rode up a few seconds ago." He indicated Red Crow, now standing quietly in the pines, his head lowered as if he were napping.

"If it wasn't you…"

Again, she looked around.

"The culprit would be gone," Tiernan said.

"How can you be sure?"

He concentrated, tested the atmosphere, then shook his head. "If anyone else was around, I would sense it. 'Tis my fey Irish blood," he explained.

Frowning at him, she tried to stand once more. And once more he moved closer, this time hesitating before touching her.

"May I offer my help?"

She thought about it for a second, then gave him her hand. Though she wasn't a small woman—only a few inches shorter than he and nicely curved—he easily pulled her up to her feet. She stood there, amber gaze taking him in, while he did the same. Pale skin, wide-spaced round eyes, high cheekbones, strong chin, full lips—a mix of the people in this state.

She was the most fascinating-looking lass he'd ever met.

"Thank you," she said. "Ella Thunder."

He grinned. "Powerful name. Tiernan McKenna. I would be a cousin to Rose Farrell."

"Farrell." As if suddenly realizing he hadn't let go of her hand, she pulled hers from his grasp and slid it behind her back. "They have a ranch a couple miles from here, right?"

So she didn't know them. "That they do. The MKF—stands for McKenna-Farrell. Aren't you from this area?"

"I used to be," she said. "I was on my way to visit the grandparents."

"On refuge land?"

"On the rez. This is a shortcut."

He could see it in her—she was definitely part, though not all, Native American. "You stopped for some reason."

"Just to look around. It's been a long time," she admitted. "I was here maybe five minutes." She checked her watch. "I must have only been out for a few minutes."

"So, in the five minutes you were here just looking around, someone decided to hurt you?"

She frowned at him again, her thick dark brows nearly pulling together. "You don't believe me?"

"Nah, nah, that's not what I was saying."

"Then what did you mean?" she asked.

"Just trying to make sense of it all. Wondering if the thing that spooked the herd was human rather than something four-footed."

"I thought it might be a cougar, too."

"So if the culprit *was* human, he could have done something to scare off the herd and then didn't want you to see his face. The question is…what was he up to?"

"I don't know. We could look around to see."

"I'm thinking you shouldn't be walking around. Or driving. You could have a concussion."

"What I have is a headache." She gave him a fierce look. "Of the human kind."

He stared down at her, tried to read her for anything unusual. Oddly, he didn't get much off her, as if she were somehow blocking him mentally. Now how was that possible? he wondered.

"Are you dizzy? Any ringing in the ears?"

"I'm a little off-center. Not exactly dizzy. More like lightheaded. No ringing." Her voice rose with her irritation. "Are you a doctor?"

He shook his head. "Working around horses, I've seen enough accidents—had a couple myself. I know the signs of a concussion. Let me get a better look at your eyes."

Before she could deny him, he lifted her chin. The contact was potent and he froze like that, not daring so much as to breathe. What was it with this woman? What was she doing to him? It took all his concentration to suck in some air and do what he meant to do. He checked her pupils—both equal in size and therefore normal—and gazed right through them, searching…searching…

A quick flash of light accompanied sharp pain and disorientation and finally the sensation of falling.

Tiernan blinked and shook his head to clear it. "I don't think you were *hit* at all—not enough to knock you out, that is."

She stiffened. "I thought you believed me."

"Turn around. Let me look at the back of your head. Please." With that she turned and he asked, "Where does it hurt?"

"Here."

Inspecting the area she'd indicated, he saw a tiny pinprick. "Just as I thought. You were darted."

"What?"

Ella flipped around to face him. A little flustered but steady enough.

"We do it with horses when necessary," Tiernan explained. "The dart contains a small explosive charge that detonates on impact and injects the drug. The dart itself often bounces off the animal."

The reason she'd recovered so quickly was that she'd barely gotten any of the drug. He inspected the ground and spotted a hint of yellow in the crushed pine needles that had been under her body. He stooped and dug out the dart, held it up with the tips of two fingers, then carefully pocketed it in his vest. Hopefully, he'd recover the attacker's fingerprints, as well.

Unarmed but for a knife sheathed on his belt, Tiernan surveyed the area, demanding assurance that the danger was over. He sensed nothing but he wasn't at ease, either.

"In a shady spot like this, the dart will flash when the explosive detonates," he went on. "That was the flash that accompanied the pain."

"I didn't tell you I saw anything."

"Of course you did or how would I know it?"

Though Ella didn't argue further, she gave him a suspicious expression. "Well, do I check out, McKenna? Can we look around now?"

Feeling only that she was slightly out of sorts, nothing more serious, Tiernan grinned and said, "Just take it slow and yell if anything doesn't feel right, Thunder." She did remind him of a thunder cloud, ready to rumble at him. "Could you tell the direction your attacker came from?"

Reorienting herself with the valley, Ella turned to the area behind her and said, "Somewhere over there."

Tiernan scanned the ground until he found some needles trampled on the forest path, no doubt by the attacker's feet. "This way. Stay close."

They moved through the trees, following the faint impressions.

Ella was the first to say, "Wait. Here the tracks go in two directions."

"Hum. I would guess the way we've been going is the way he retreated, but he came from the northeast. Must've seen or heard you and decided to investigate."

"For someone who isn't from here, you have a good sense of direction."

"Internal compass."

"Because you're fey."

Tiernan merely grinned at her and moved along.

The grin didn't last long. As he stepped through the trees onto red earth and rock, his senses picked up once more. Something had happened here. Something bad. Foreboding filled him as he scanned the ground, noted that there were no footprints. Had whoever walked here purposely obliterated them? Someone had been here, of that he was certain. He felt remnants of the human presence.

"Dead end," Ella said, coming up behind him.

"I don't think so."

Stepping forward, he looked across the valley, trying to find the spot he'd been in when the horses had fled. But it wasn't visible. So whatever had happened here, he wouldn't have been able to see....

"What are you doing?" Ella asked, her hand suddenly grabbing his arm.

Tiernan stopped just short of the cliff's edge. He hadn't

even realized how close he'd gotten. What he did realize was that his pulse was humming, his gut was tightening. He simply couldn't decide if it was because of whatever happened here…or because of Ella touching him.

He removed his arm and the humming faded, the tightening eased.

And then, disturbed by the sensations he'd just experienced, he took that last step forward and looked down only to have the nightmare of his past flash back at him.

Chapter Two

Tiernan's back straightened and he removed his hat—crushing it to his chest—and lowered his head, causing Ella to hesitate from stepping forward.

"What is it?" she asked.

"We need to get back to refuge headquarters, call the authorities."

He turned from the edge of the cliff and indicated they should go back the way they came. His movements were stiff, his face pale. There was something deeply wrong here, she could sense it. Tiernan McKenna was an attractive man—dark reddish brown hair framing a handsome, boyish face. The tight line of his wide, unsmiling mouth and the shadowed expression in his thick-lashed green eyes told her it wasn't good…but she wasn't leaving until she saw for herself.

When Ella stepped forward, he put an arm out to stop her. She didn't say anything, just met his gaze, making her intent clear by staying fast. He changed his stance, moved away from her, and she was about to take that last step when she glanced down and saw the scratching in the earth—a long line with an inverted V halfway through it.

The last time she'd seen that sign had been on Father's forehead right before he'd died.

Her chest suddenly squeezing tight, she couldn't move for a moment. Someone had scratched the raven's track purposely as a warning.

Someone malevolent.

Reluctantly now, her stomach clenching, she looked over the edge, her gaze going straight to the body sprawled on a ledge thirty or so feet below.

He lay so still he almost looked like he was asleep—a man, young, copper-skinned, probably Lakota—but his head was twisted unnaturally and his dark eyes were open, vacant. Though she couldn't see from such a distance, she instinctively sensed his eyes were already clouded with death.

She closed her own eyes and said a silent prayer for the poor man's soul.

"Do you know him?" Tiernan asked.

"I—I'm not sure." She blinked her eyes open and looked again. "It's been too many years."

She focused on the man, opened her mind, calling in vain to the elements to guide her. No matter how hard she tried, the power remained unresponsive. It had been too long since her father had taught her....

Tiernan broke into her thoughts with a soft, "Hey."

Suddenly the summer day seemed cold and the fitful wind iced over her. As if he could sense that, he wrapped an arm lightly around her shoulders; this time, she accepted his touch and, despite herself, leaned into his warmth.

That she'd nearly witnessed a murder, nearly had seen the killer, made her shudder inside. It scared up too horrible a memory.

"C'mon, let's get you away from here," Tiernan said, leading her back the way they came. "I'll get you to headquarters, then call the authorities. Let them handle this."

"I—I have a cell—"

"As do I, for all the good it'll do us in this area. I've never been able to scare up a signal in this part of the mountain."

"The grandparents—they're expecting me."

"You can call them on a land phone, can you not?" When she nodded, he said, "The authorities will want to take our statements."

Ella knew that to be true, even as she knew she couldn't be completely truthful. If she told anyone other than the grandparents about the raven's track she'd seen in the earth, they would laugh at her, treat her like she was primitive. Foolish.

Maybe, but memory told another story.

The last time she'd seen that sign Father had been burned to death!

Despite Tiernan's trying to take care of her, Ella insisted on driving herself to refuge headquarters. She hated feeling out of control. When they arrived at the refuge, he jumped out of his truck and was at the door of her SUV practically before she could open it.

"Come on, let's get you inside," he said, trying to take her arm.

This time she avoided him. "Thanks anyway, but I'm fine on my own."

Reception was a large room that held a seating area on one side, a work area on the other. The place was empty, so Ella crossed the planked floor and threw herself into one of the chairs with a leather base and upholstered cushions just to steady herself.

"Are you all right?"

"As all right as anyone can be after finding a body, I guess." She looked over to the desk and noted the telephone. "Do you want to call the authorities or shall I?"

"A deputy and an ambulance are already on the way here. I was able to scare up a signal on my cell a half mile back and so called it in."

ook up the second floor, a log addition to the original stone single-floor building. A balcony fronted the second floor, an enclosed porch and patio backed the first. The spare room and bath that would be his for the summer were just off the kitchen.

Kate and her family had to come downstairs for meals, which was just as well since Kate and Chase ate, slept and lived their jobs anyway. Maggie spent as much time with her grandmother as she did at home. Though Chase had been here, as soon as the sheriff's men left, he went to check on the herd, to make sure no one had messed with his mustangs.

Kate caught up to Tiernan. "I don't need to be psychic to see the way you were looking at Ella the whole time she was here."

Heading across the reception area, he said, "I felt sorry for her is all."

"Maybe. But there's something else."

"I have no interest in women." Realizing what he'd just said, Tiernan stopped dead in his tracks and clarified. "That is, in pursuing a relationship with one."

"Because you'll go back to Ireland and you fear she won't want to go with you?"

"Because I cannot ever fall in love."

Kate snorted. "Is this some kind of impairment you're laiming?"

"More like a dark legacy. You should understand that nce your side of the McKennas have had to deal with a gacy of your own."

He entered the kitchen. Kate followed, quickly set Maggie wn in her corner playpen, then got in front of him.

"Whoa." Green eyes wide, red hair seeming electrified, she d, "You can't just make such a provocative statement and n walk off. Explain!"

Now he'd gone and done it. Tiernan hung his head. He'd ever discussed the secret with immediate family, his

"The sheriff's office?"

"Who else?"

He hadn't been around long enough to know the po of crimes dealing with the Lakota. The tribal police woul called in when one of her own was involved, the FBI whe involved murder.

Let the sheriff's deputy sort it all out, she thought, wishi she had never stopped to take in the scenery. All she neede was to be involved with another murder.

HOURS LATER, AFTER the body was retrieved, after they both gave their stories to a sheriff's deputy who'd sounded skeptical when Tiernan suggested murder, after a medic had checked over Ella and had drawn her blood to test for drugs, Ella was then free to head to her grandparents' home.

Tiernan was sorry to see her go. Though he didn't reason it out, he watched her SUV drive off until it disappeared in the distance.

At which point, he realized Kate was studying him. She balanced her little girl—eight-month-old Maggie, otherwise known as Magpie—on her hip and just gave him a loo went right through him.

"What?" he asked, concentrating on Maggie, wh cooing at him and staring, too. Smiling into her brigh McKenna eyes, he brushed her chubby cheek with hi and got a peal of laughter from her.

"You have a thing for Ella Thunder," Kate state

Tiernan sobered. "And here I was thinking yo abilities were reserved for your horses."

He turned away and went inside, planning himself a mug of coffee.

Headquarters was really part of Kate an Maggie's home. Their living quarters, other tha brothers mostly, because they were all at risk. He supposed Kate was family and it wouldn't hurt to tell her.

"Can I at least get coffee first?" He needed something to bolster himself before getting into it.

Kate stepped aside. "Pour one for me, too."

As Tiernan picked up the pot, he said, "My great-grandfather Donal was something of a ladies' man. He involved himself with the wrong woman, then left her to marry the one he fell in love with. The wrong woman claimed to be half faerie and all witch. And it must be true, because she put a love curse on all Donal's descendants. We are destined to love...but if we act upon our feelings—physically, that is—we will somehow put the one we love in mortal danger."

"Sounds like the ravings of a woman scorned."

"Except 'tis a prophecy that's come true many times over the decades."

"Oh, come on," Kate said, though she didn't sound as skeptical as one might think she should be.

"Truly. My grandfather lost my grandmother to a horse-riding accident soon after she gave birth to my da. My great-aunt lost her beloved in a bank robbery. My uncle lost his new wife to a speeding car...."

Though he'd only been seven at the time, Tiernan could still see the whole incident in his mind, a scene that he couldn't erase, because he'd been with Aunt Megan—she'd traded her own life for his. Nightmares of her death had followed him all his life. That he couldn't put the incident behind him after so many years made him think it was because he needed to atone for what happened. This more than anything had convinced him the prophecy was true.

"And the list goes on," he said through the lump wedged in his throat. "I can do without that kind of doom hanging over my head."

"But those could have been coincidences," Kate argued. "They all had children, right?"

"Eventually, because they settled for someone who wouldn't invoke the witch's curse. Unfortunately, though the spouse may survive, the prophecy doesn't depend on love to infect the next generation."

Kate frowned. "Sounds really sad to me, Tiernan…whether it's settling…or living alone out of fear—"

He interrupted. "There are worse things." How could a man live with himself if he caused his woman's death? he wondered, knowing how his aunt's death had crushed Uncle Ross. Better never to love at all. "Now, I would appreciate your telling me about the new job with the film company."

Even as he changed the subject, Tiernan remembered that moment on the cliff when Ella had grabbed his arm and something disturbing had passed through him. Just his response to an attractive woman, he told himself. After the tragedies he'd seen happen to love-happy people he cared about—after seeing Aunt Megan lying still and cold and broken on the pavement and knowing there would be no justice for her death—he could never let it be more.

Not a problem since he probably would never see the lovely Ella Thunder again.

TRYING TO KEEP herself relaxed and entertained by thoughts of Tiernan McKenna with his mesmerizing green eyes, seductive Irish lilt and fascinating way of getting to her with just a touch, Ella drove through the rez. Despite her determination, a memory of her father in his last moments came back to her, cramped her stomach and pushed Tiernan out of mind.

Ella took a deep breath and shook away the vision as she drove past sad-looking houses and trailers, kids shrieking as they played in the dirt, their imaginations turning junk into toys. Though the rez was small in size, with residences mostly scattered far and wide over the land—only a few dozen had been built around the center of town—Grandmother had written that the houses and trailers were overcrowded, that there were too many people and not enough money.

Looking around, Ella could see it for herself. Though she didn't remember the rez looking so worn, she supposed it always had been. Things always looked different through the eyes of youth.

Other than work provided by the casino or general store or gas station, or for the tribal police or council, there simply weren't enough jobs on the rez. People had to drive into Bitter Creek or Custer or to one of the farther towns or cities to find work. She knew the film company was not only paying the rez for using their land and horses, but hiring many of the Lakota to do odd jobs or to be extras in the movie. A few had even been given speaking parts. Hopefully enough money would be infused into the rez to kick-start the economy here.

The first building of any notable size that she passed was the casino. And then the government offices. A few dozen homes were scattered around the rez's center.

Ella drove straight to what used to be her own home and left the SUV, her stomach in knots. The air outside was thick, hard to breathe, her mounting tension no doubt the cause.

Then the door opened, and a small woman in long skirts and a bleached cotton shirt shuffled out. Her hair was pure white now, her skin like elephant's hide. Dina Thunder was an old seventy-one. And seventy-one *was* old for the rez, where people rarely survived their sixties. The smile that curved Grandmother's lips and lit her eyes exactly as Ella remembered made her a welcoming committee of one.

"My Ella!"

Grandmother held up her arms and Ella couldn't help but

notice the arthritic joints in her hands. When she stooped to hug Ella, Ella was aware of how fragile the elderly woman had become despite the roundness of her figure. Grandmother held on to her as if she might never let go.

A white-haired man stood in the doorway—Grandfather. Samuel Thunder was still an imposing figure, his face a carved reminder of her own ancestry. His eyes were unfocused, his head cocked slightly as if he were trying to get a sideways look at her.

Ella knew eye disease hampered Grandfather from making out details, such as her features, but he could get impressions, and whatever he did see made him smile, showing off his gold tooth. She went to him and hugged him, too. She used to think Grandfather was so tall, like Father, but now she was nearly his equal.

"Grandfather, I missed you."

"You are a woman now, Ella. Strong and beautiful, Joseph's true daughter."

"I hope this is so."

"Can you eat?" Grandmother asked.

"I'm starving."

"Inside with you."

The walls were painted white, better to show off the collection of woven baskets that surrounded the combination living and dining room. A threadbare rug covered part of the planked floor, and a bow and arrow perched over the stone fireplace.

Ella inhaled the luscious aroma coming from the stove and sighed—the memory of Grandmother's cooking kicking in. "There's no bison stew as good as yours." Her mouth was already watering.

"I made a corn pudding and baked pumpkin, too. And blueberry Wojapi to go with the fry bread."

As they ate, they caught up on the missing years, concentrating on the positive rather than dwelling on the dark past that sent Ella, her mother and sister, Miranda, fleeing to the white world. A past from which her mother had never recovered. The grandparents wanted to know every detail about Ella's work as a teacher of history, especially of *their* history.

"We have your book on the table by the couch so everyone who comes here can see it," Grandmother told her.

"Your father would be proud of you," Grandfather said. "Your returning to us shows that you are as fierce a warrior as he was."

Ella's pulse fluttered and her chest tightened. "Not fierce. The movie interested me... I couldn't resist. A couple of weeks here seemed perfect."

The grandparents exchanged looks that told Ella they didn't accept that. Believers in fate, they would assume her presence had been guided by her animal spirit. While the film had delivered her, they would be convinced she was here for something more.

When they finished eating, Grandfather went outside to sit and to puff on his pipe, and Ella began clearing the table.

"It is so good to have you home, Ella."

"Only for a few weeks, Grandmother. Only for the movie. This isn't my home anymore."

"This is where you are needed." Grandmother hesitated only for a moment before saying, "We have no shaman. No one will practice here after what happened to Joseph."

"I'm not a shaman."

*It is time...*whispered through Ella's head, but she instantly denied it.

Time for what? To give the people hope? Or to give hope to herself?

Ella pushed back the confusion. She reminded herself that she was just here for a summer job.

"Please, Granddaughter, the people need a spiritual leader. Do it for your grandfather and me—for your father—so that the legacy of the elders continues."

The plea got to Ella—Grandmother had never asked anything of her before. While Ella remembered the tenets of her father's beliefs and powers, she wasn't sure she could actually execute them. Furthermore, even if it was something she *wanted* to do, she feared what might happen if she tried. She'd shut herself off from calling on the elements for fifteen years because Father had proved using abilities people didn't understand was too dangerous, and she wasn't about to embrace the danger again.

Still, having to deny the elderly woman made her feel bad. "I *can't* help anyone, Grandmother. I am no medicine woman. And I don't know if I remember enough of what Father taught me."

"Talk to Nathan. *He* remembers."

The tight, scarred skin on her arm twitched and Ella smoothed the cotton sleeve covering it. Part of her thanked her cousin for saving her. Part of her blamed him for letting her live burn- and memory-scarred.

Pausing a few seconds, she then asked, "So Nathan turned his back on shamanism?"

Grandmother nodded. "He has other interests that concern our people."

"What kind of interests?"

"He's become an activist. He's part of First Nation."

Ella knew about the long-standing activist group First Nation—a group that believed the Lakota should withdraw from all treaties with the United States and should reclaim the *Paha Sapa* for The People. *Paha Sapa*—the heart of everything that is—otherwise known as the Black Hills, Ella thought. Father had taught her the mountain held great power that needed to be respected. She knew that three decades ago, a federal court had agreed that in taking the land to mine gold in the 1870s, Custer had broken the treaty. The court had awarded the Lakota money that had now amassed to nearly a billion dollars. The Lakota were unwilling to trade their rights to the land for money. They didn't believe in buying or selling the earth they walked upon.

Ella said, "I don't think the U.S. government is ever going to give the land back to The People." Her band was lucky to have been awarded a small reservation on one edge of the mountain, a lush piece of land compared to Pine Ridge, the next closest reservation on the Badlands.

"No. But I fear what First Nation might do to reclaim land they believe belongs to us," Grandmother said. "We don't need more war. Poverty and disease already take their toll on The People. What we need is someone who can heal the ills, not increase them."

Doing the dishes gave Ella time to consider Grandmother's words, as scary as it was for her.

Why had she come here if not to get involved with The People? an inner voice asked. Her working with the movie company and then coming back to the rez just to sleep would prove nothing.

She needed contact...knowledge...closure.

She needed to know the real reason that Father had died.

She needed to find the villain who was responsible and see that he was punished.

Chapter Three

Early the next morning, Ella left the house for her SUV, ready to head out to the film set and meet with Jane Grant. They'd only spoken on the phone or via e-mails, so she was a little anxious to get together with the producer in person. She was about to open the vehicle door when she sensed interested eyes on the back of her neck.

Turning, she locked gazes with a man standing just behind her. His eyes were dark and he had long black hair, a braid in the front decorated with strips of beading and feathers. His features had matured, his body filled out, but she had no doubt as to his identity. She remembered what Grandmother had told her about him the night before. Her stomach tightened as she nodded to her cousin.

"Nathan."

His expression serious, Nathan Lantero stepped closer so that she could see that he was wearing a beaded necklace with his totem, a buffalo cast in gold. Ella couldn't help but be surprised—it looked like real gold, an unbelievable luxury amidst so much poverty. She remembered when they were kids, they would secretly search the abandoned mines in hope of finding gold. Now it looked like Nathan had, if not in the way they'd imagined.

What kind of work had he been able to get to earn it? she wondered.

"I heard you left the *Wasi'chu,* Ella. I couldn't help but wonder why, after all this time."

He almost sounded disapproving, she thought, as if he thought she should have stayed with her mother's people. *Wasi'chu* was used as reference to the White Man, but she suspected as an activist, Nathan used it in its newer negative context, to describe a human condition based on exploitation. That he'd used it in reference to *her* made her stomach knot and her pulse rush a little faster.

Her back up, Ella said, "An odd question considering you lived with your father's people for years." Both her father and his mother had married outside the Lakota. "Besides, I have roots here."

"You had a nightmare here."

"Nightmares follow wherever you go," she said, knowing this to be true. "No place is safe."

Nathan nodded, and Ella knew he, too, had felt her father's death. He'd been one of the family. Almost like a brother to her. Even so, she hadn't really spoken to him since the day her father was murdered.

Ella wanted in the worst way to ply her cousin with questions about the past. Perhaps he could help her sort it all out. Not now, though. No time—she had that meeting. Besides, with that attitude, Nathan surely wouldn't be receptive to anything she wanted.

Still, she needed to try to make peace between them.

"I...I never thanked you for trying to help Father...and me."

"Joseph was my teacher and my uncle. He was like a father to me, as well."

A grief-stricken thirteen-year-old, Ella had placed blame on him. Analytically, she now recognized Nathan had not only saved her from disfigurement or worse, but he'd done what he could for her father. Of course, emotions had no logic, and back then, hers had been out of control.

"I'm sorry I was so horrible to you after…."

"So there are no hard feelings?"

"For you? No, of course not," she said. "You and Leonard Hawkins tried to stop what happened. Not everyone went along with the crowd."

"What about those who did?" He glanced back as if looking over a now-invisible angry crowd, when no one even walked within sight of the house. "Can you forgive and forget?" he asked, turning back to search her face.

Ella had no answer. She wanted to be able to forgive—holding hatred in her heart could make her as sick as any disease—but she simply didn't know if she could look at the past through a softer lens.

"Maybe that's why I'm here—to find out if forgiving is possible."

"I hope that's true."

But she could tell he didn't quite believe her. His thick brows were furrowed, and his full mouth pulled tight. More important, she felt his doubt come at her in palpable waves.

Doubt and something else…something darker…something that made her take a step back and jam her elbow into the car.

Ignoring the shot of pain, she asked, "What is it you fear, Nathan?"

"Revenge is a strong need."

"You think *I* would deliberately hurt others?" Or did he mean himself?

"I don't know you anymore, Ella."

"Nor I you." Suddenly wanting to put some distance between herself and her cousin, Ella looked away from him and swung open the door of the SUV, but hesitated before getting in. Being rude wouldn't earn his help in the future. "I need to go now or I'll be late to an appointment."

"Then I'll probably see you on the set."

Ella supposed she shouldn't be surprised that Nathan knew she was working on the film. Undoubtedly Grandmother had told him.

What was he going to be doing there? Working or protesting?

"Did you get a speaking part?"

He stared at her for a moment, making her shift uncomfortably as she wondered what was going through his head.

Then he said, "Only speaking to the horses from the rez. I'm moving some into a pasture near the Sioux village set this morning."

"I'll see you there, then."

Nathan gave her a ghost of a smile and backed off as she climbed into the driver's seat. But he didn't turn away.

Considering Nathan was part of an activist group trying to regain the Black Hills for The People, Ella found it odd that he would want to have anything to do with the movie. Then again, money was money and he surely needed to make a living somehow.

After driving off, Ella kept glancing into her rearview mirror. Nathan was there, still watching her, until she turned the corner.

It was only then that she relaxed.

What the heck?

Why had he been giving off such a weird vibe, like he didn't want her there?

Lord, who knew? Maybe he considered her *Wasi'chu.* Maybe he resented the work she'd gotten, especially her being the consultant for the spiritual scenes. Though he was no shaman, Nathan *had* been one of Father's apprentices. Grandmother said he remembered. Perhaps he'd wanted to be the consultant and resented the lucrative work going to someone who'd spent the last half of her life living in the white world.

Maybe he had a point.

As she drove, Ella let her thoughts stray back to the day before. It was still too early to call the sheriff's office—she doubted they would know anything until later. If she didn't hear anything by midafternoon, she would call for an update.

She turned onto a gravel road that cut between reservation and refuge and remembered her encounter with Tiernan McKenna, whose people owned this land. Without calling it up, she could see his handsome Irish face. The way he looked at her with such concern…the way his expression changed with an injection of humor.

And then she remembered the nonverbal connection between them. The connection had been made several times, in different ways. She'd felt him, as if she could sense him inside her somehow. Like nothing she'd ever felt before, she thought. Tiernan seemed strangely intuitive—"Irish fey" he'd called it jokingly. For some reason, Ella thought it was more than that, something more compelling, perhaps even dark. The more she considered it, the more edgy she became.

One didn't have to be a Native American shaman to have powers that the average person could only imagine. Ireland was a land of fables. But perhaps there was more fact than fiction to the magic claimed by the Irish.

Ella shuddered at the possibilities.

Only here for a few weeks, she might never see Tiernan McKenna again.

Good thing…

BEFORE LEAVING FOR the set, Tiernan called the sheriff's office and asked for the deputy who'd taken his statement. He'd been up half the night remembering…and worrying.

"We determined Harold Walks Tall's death was accidental," the deputy said.

Familiar words tore through him.

Though he was certain that was not true, Tiernan made no rash claims as he once had. He endeavored to stay calm, focused, logical.

"Are you certain the man wasn't darted?"

"No markings on him, no tranquilizer or other drugs in his system."

"Then how do you explain what happened to Ella Thunder?" Tiernan asked, wondering if she had any lingering ill effects from the drug.

The attack on Ella being the *only* reason he was thinking of her at all.

"Coincidence?" the deputy responded. "Look, probably some hunter was out there and saw movement through the trees and thought she was a deer. When he realized his mistake, he took off. It don't make him a nice person, but it don't make him a criminal, either."

Tiernan guessed the assumption was logical given what the authorities had to go on, but remembering the way his psychic instincts had been aroused—something he couldn't prove and therefore wouldn't share. He was certain the fall was no accident. It wasn't the first time he'd been privy to such a mistake in a death investigation. Having had experience trying to convince the authorities they were wrong, he knew it was an exercise in futility.

"Why would a hunter use a tranquilizer rather than a bullet to bring down an animal?" Tiernan asked.

The deputy coughed and hemmed and hawed. "Can't really say why…."

Tiernan knew arguing would be a waste of energy. Even so, he asked, "What about the dart itself?"

"No fingerprints." The deputy was starting to sound really uncomfortable. "Look, the lady is okay, which is what really matters, right? Searching for someone who made a mistake would be a waste of manpower."

The lack of resolution lay heavily on Tiernan's mind as he drove out to the set, taking the truck that Kate had said was his as long as the job lasted. He knew what he knew, but it was nothing he could prove, and it was none of his business anyway, he thought.

Not like the last time.

So why was he so focused on it? Focused on a lass he didn't even know?

He tried to get it—*her*—out of mind and concentrate on the job at hand as he approached the shooting location. Some carpenters were at work on one of the buildings, a handful of men surrounding a couple of cameras looked as if they were trying to decide where to set up and extras and production staff milled about.

Driving straight to the double-wide marked as the office, Tiernan went in search of Doug Holloway, the first assistant director, who would be his supervisor.

Doug turned out to be a small man both in height and weight. His thick sandy hair was tied back in a ponytail and his pale blue eyes hid behind a pair of round tortoiseshell glasses. He was young—twentysomething—and fast talking.

"I'm not a horse expert—that would be you—so I'll give you the shooting schedule with the number of horses I need. It's up to you to have them ready to ride on time every day according to schedule. Got it?"

"That I do," Tiernan said, taking the folder from Doug and browsing the contents. "What about the horses from the reservation?"

"Not your headache. You'll coordinate with a Lakota—

Nathan Lantero—who should be bringing in the reservation's horses anytime now."

Closing the folder, Tiernan said, "Looks like I'd better do the same since you'll need some of those horses first thing in the morning. Which pasture do I use?"

Doug shrugged. "First come, first served. Both have trailers parked outside the gates to use as tack rooms. Just let me know when you're finished setting up."

"Will do."

An all-day job, Tiernan thought, but one better than rounding up cattle. Until he'd come here, horses had been his life. Hoping Kate or Chase could help him for a few hours, he left the trailer and made for the truck. He'd barely reached the parking lot when he spotted the familiar, green SUV. He turned back toward the set to look for Ella, but he didn't see her. He was getting that odd feeling again, that sense of connection. The prophecy came immediately to mind, and Tiernan told himself that it would be best for him to stay away from the woman.

What was Ella doing here in the first place? he wondered.

Was she an extra? Or had she simply come along with a friend or relative for the experience?

Whatever the reason, he intended to avoid her and hoped their paths wouldn't cross when he returned with the herd.

"WHY DOES IT have to be a cottonwood?" Jane Grant asked. "I don't understand why any tree wouldn't do."

They were discussing the Sundance to be shot in the next few days and Ella wanted the scene to be as authentic as possible. They'd been at it all day and this was the last planning detail that needed attention.

"Well, it doesn't. You could use another tree, but the cottonwood is sacred to the Lakota," Ella told her. "The leaves are shaped in the conical pattern of the tipi. And an upper limb cut crosswise will show a five-pointed star that represents the Great Spirit. If you want the scene to be truly authentic…."

"All right, then, a cottonwood it is." Jane made a note of it on her laptop. "I'll get someone on it before we break for the day."

While intelligent and efficient, Jane Grant seemed too young, not even thirty years old, to be a producer of a major motion picture. Her short blond hair was spiked, her medium-length fingernails painted the same dark blue as her tight pants. She wore a hand-worked leather halter top and matching boots…with three-inch heels. Ella wondered how in the world she could walk in those on such uneven ground without twisting an ankle.

When Jane looked up and closed the lid of her laptop, Ella said, "I appreciate your taking the details of our ceremony so seriously. Rituals need to be observed properly so the gods bestow the blessings of life on The People."

Jane nodded. "All right. I appreciate your willingness to work with me. Not all Lakota are as cooperative."

Ella's only response was a smile.

"Well, that finishes your work for the day," Jane said. "Meet me here in the morning. Ten should be fine. I'd like you to look over everything before we start shooting."

Ella got to her feet. "Good, I'll see you then."

As she left the trailer, a ruckus caught her attention—stomping hoofbeats accompanied by sharp whistles. Horses, twenty or so, were being driven toward the pasture on the set. Ella couldn't help but be drawn toward the activity. And when she spotted Tiernan McKenna bringing up the rear of the herd, her step quickened. His cousin Kate remained at the gate and shooed the horses through.

Then, remembering her earlier thoughts about Tiernan and Irish magic, Ella slowed and thought twice about approaching him. What in the world was she doing?

Too late. Tiernan spotted her. Not knowing what else to do, she waved and indicated she wanted to talk to him. Maybe he knew something about the murder—a good enough reason for her interest.

Tiernan and Kate quickly got the horses into the fenced pasture. He bent over to say something to his cousin, who grinned at him and hit him in the arm as if she were teasing. *Now, what was that about?*

Then Tiernan turned his gelding in her direction, and Ella felt her pulse rush a little faster. Behind him, Kate watched, waved to Ella, then took off the way she'd come. His expression sober, Tiernan stopped the horse directly in front of her but didn't dismount.

Feeling her face grow warm, Ella looked up at him and said, "I didn't know you were working on the set."

"That would make two of us. Are you just visiting or are you one of the actresses?"

"Actress?" Ella couldn't help but laugh at that. She'd made the same mistake with Nathan earlier. "I couldn't act my way out of a paper bag. I'm just doing a little consulting work. The producer wants to get the Lakota scenes dealing with spirituality right. I'll only be here for a couple of weeks." She realized that, despite her earlier thoughts, she'd relaxed while talking to Tiernan. His expression had softened, as well. "So you're wrangling the horses?"

"The ones from both the family ranch and the refuge. Not the reservation horses."

"No, that would be my cousin."

"Cousin?" His forehead pulled into a frown. "Do I detect some tension there?"

"Nathan can be difficult," Ella said, then admitted, "We had words earlier."

"'Tis a shame."

She shrugged. "The reason I stopped you…have you heard anything about what happened yesterday?"

"It seems that Harold Walks Tall's death was declared an accident."

"No! That can't be right!"

"I don't believe it, either. But apparently they found no drug in his system."

"What about what happened to me?"

"The deputy put it to a hunter making a mistake, thinking he was aiming at an animal. A waste of time 'twould be going after someone who merely made a mistake."

She didn't miss the sarcasm in his voice. "That was no more a mistake than Harold Walks Tall's death was an accident!"

"'Tis not *me* you need to convince."

"There's just no way to prove it," Ella said.

No easy way.

No way she wanted to take.

All her instincts had been aroused by the incident. Before she'd known there was a body, she'd sensed the darkness and danger…and then she'd seen the raven's track in the earth. But those were all things she was unwilling to talk about. Things that could raise suspicions. Things that could get a person killed.

Forcing the image of Father as she'd seen him last out of her mind, Ella was about to suggest it would be best to leave it alone when the thunder of hooves caught her attention again. She looked past Tiernan to see another herd of horses heading toward the fenced pastures.

"Looks like Nathan is here." Her cousin and two other men from the rez were bringing in the herd.

"I should be introducing myself, then. Forge a bond since we shall be working together."

"I'm not sure that's possible. Even though Nathan went away to university and lived in the white world for years, he returned to his mother's people and the rez. He's become something of an activist, part of a group that wants to dissolve treaties and take back the Black Hills for the Lakota."

"Could that happen?"

"What reason would a powerful government have to give over settled and valuable land?"

"Aye, that I understand. Hopefully it won't cause troubles here."

"Hopefully."

"Maybe you ought to come with me, do the introductions."

Ella glanced over at the herd her cousin had brought. Nathan was behind the last of the horses to go into the pasture. One of his men swung closed the gate and latched it.

"Looks like it's too late."

"Not if you ride with me." Tiernan removed his left foot from the stirrup. "Get on."

Ella hesitated but Tiernan gestured for her to mount behind him. Tossing caution to the wind, she slipped her foot into the stirrup and bounced upward, catching him around the waist to anchor herself as she threw her free leg over the horse's back.

He took off immediately, and as her breasts pressed into his back, Ella realized her mistake. Her head went light and her pulse started to race and she felt that uncomfortable connection with him yet again. And from the way he suddenly stiffened in the saddle, she expected he felt it, too.

What did this mean? Her being light-headed and disconnected from everything but him? She felt as if she were converging with him somehow—not here, but on another plane.

Distracted by the discomfort and weird thoughts, Ella didn't realize one of Nathan's men was yelling about something in Lakota until Tiernan stopped near the pastures. Even though she was an expert in Lakota history, she'd spoken nothing but English since leaving the rez. Even so, she caught some of the words. Something about a curse. Then the man looked her way and his face curdled in contempt. She didn't recognize him, but he pointed at her and said she was the one.

"What's going on?" Tiernan asked.

"I—I don't know."

And then she did. Scratched into the fence posts that joined the two pastures was a raven's track.

Chapter Four

"What is he talking about?" Tiernan asked, glancing back to see that Ella's face had gone white.

"Superstition," she said, but he knew there was more to it than she was willing to admit.

"Jacob, back to the rez," Ella's cousin ordered.

Jacob kept his eyes on Ella as he backed up and got hold of his horse. He kept staring at her even as he mounted and rode off.

Tiernan could feel Ella's horror. Her arms were still wound around his waist. He had that feeling again, same as the day before, something he didn't want to recognize. Still, sensing she was close to panicking, he tried to comfort her by placing his free arm over hers and clasping one of her hands. And then he called up peaceful thoughts and concentrated on that and gradually felt her calm down.

An imposing figure, Nathan Lantero walked over to them, stopping near Ella. "Don't worry about Jacob," he told her. "I'll speak with him."

"Do you think it will do any good?"

"It's only a sign, Ella. Nothing bad happened. What will he be able to tell The People? Nothing."

"I hope you're right."

Not wanting to dismount and break the fragile bond he had with Ella, Tiernan stayed fast as he addressed the other horseman.

"Looks like you and I will be working together, wrangling horses for this film. Tiernan McKenna." He held out his hand for a shake.

Dark eyes seared him as if trying to look through him, to make him retreat, or at least look away first. Tiernan didn't so much as shift in the saddle. There was something to this Nathan beyond what he could see, only he couldn't put his finger on what. He trusted his instincts, though—psychic or otherwise—and they were all on alert.

Finally, the other man reached out and took his hand. "Nathan Lantero. Ella's cousin, though she's probably already told you who I am. What's an Irishman doing in the wilds of South Dakota?"

"Working with horses, same as I would do back home," Tiernan said, getting everything and yet nothing from the contact with the man, as if Nathan were blocking him. "Well, in a manner of speaking," he qualified. "In Ireland I trained Thoroughbreds. And I'm here in this area because the Farrells are blood."

"Good people," Nathan said, pulling his hand free. "I used to work for Kate's husband, Chase, on the refuge."

"But you quit?"

"I had more pressing interests."

Though his curiosity was piqued, Tiernan didn't ask Nathan to explain what those interests might be. "I shall be seeing you, then." He nodded to one of the trailers. "Right now, I need to be getting the tack shop set up."

Nathan simply inclined his head.

Tipping his hat in return, Tiernan signaled Red Crow to go back the way they'd come. He waited a bit before saying to Ella, "So your cousin worked for the refuge."

"I didn't even know that. He was barely eighteen when Mother brought us back to Sioux Falls, and then Grandmother said he went to California, to go to school and to live with his father's people."

"But he returned here. His pressing interests in the Black Hills?"

Ella didn't look thrilled about the fact. Tiernan supposed she feared the activists could start a war over their holy land. He hoped not. He hadn't forgotten the troubles in Ireland. He wouldn't wish that violence and fear on anyone.

As they approached the trailers, he asked, "Where should I drop you?"

"The parking lot would be best since I was on my way out when I saw you."

When Ella dismounted near her SUV, Tiernan felt an inexplicable sense of loss. He couldn't say why, but he wasn't ready to let her go.

"I'm wondering if we could get together later," he said. "Maybe have a drink." When her expression shifted to one of caution, as if she was searching for reasons to decline, he wheedled, "I think we should talk more about what happened yesterday, don't you? Besides, I wouldn't be knowing anyone here but relatives."

Ella's expression cleared. "Sure. A drink. I could meet you in town this evening about eight? A place called Red Butte Saloon."

"I will be there."

Tiernan smiled down at Ella and he kept himself from giving her a wink. She reminded him of a deer poised to flee at the slightest hint of danger.

There was danger enough around them—he was certain of that, no matter what the deputy had claimed—reason enough for him to keep Ella close.

ELLA CENTERED HERSELF before entering. The Red Butte Saloon had a purposely Old West feel and its bar was of black walnut, massive and hand-carved, a long mirror along the back wall making the place look twice as big. The walls themselves were lined with wood paneling and decorated with Western and Native American memorabilia.

Part of Ella wished that Tiernan wouldn't be there, while another part looked forward to seeing him again. Beyond his being attractive and charming—he was definitely both—he interested her and she couldn't quite say why.

Tiernan had gotten there before her and didn't see her come in. He stood at the bar, beer in hand, with a group of men. She doubted he knew them—at least he'd *said* he only had family here—but they were talking and laughing as if they were old friends. She guessed he could charm men, too.

Watching Tiernan—his relaxed style, his genuine smile, his easy laugh—Ella wondered how she could have thought him so threatening the first time they'd met.

As she made her way toward him, her pulse threaded unevenly. She was here for a drink, nothing more. How could there be more with her returning to Sioux Falls in a couple of weeks? So why the expectation, the catch in her breath, the edgy sense of something about to happen?

Tiernan glanced her way, and when he saw her, locked his gaze with hers. The space around them dissolved into nothingness. She felt as if he could see inside her...as if she should be able to see inside him. The closer she got, the more intense the connection.

And then he reached out and touched her and she simply lost the ability to breathe.

"So you came," he said, his voice warm. "I was worried you would change your mind."

"I—I almost did," she choked out.

"'Tis glad I am that you thought twice on the matter," he said, his voice whiskey smooth. "What will you have to drink?"

"A red beer."

Tiernan turned to the bartender and handed him some money. "The lady wants a red." The bartender quickly filled a mug and handed it to Tiernan, who indicated a dark corner. "We'll just be taking ourselves to that booth."

"Tina will be your waitress. I'll have her check on you in a while."

With a beer in each hand, Tiernan nodded to him, and indicated Ella should take the lead. Separating from the crowd, she felt her pulse rush a little faster. It wasn't like she was going to be alone with the man, but she couldn't help her reaction. There was something powerful about him…something so deeply magnetic that she couldn't deny it.

She slid into one side of the booth as Tiernan set down the two mugs. Then she slid her beer closer and fingered the icy glass as he sat opposite.

"To smooth sailing on the set," Tiernan said, raising his mug. He waited until they'd both taken a sip before saying, "So define *superstition* for me."

Warmth rose in her face as she remembered evading him earlier. "There was a raven's track carved into one of the fence posts on the pasture. That man, Jacob, thought it meant a sign of something bad about to happen."

"I saw it, the same as in the earth where Harold Walks Tall fell to his death."

"You saw that one, too?" She gasped. "Why didn't you say anything?"

"Why didn't *you?*"

"Not everyone believes in these signs. People who weren't brought up on the rez tend to think of them as superstition. They don't give them credence, perhaps even think those who do are foolish," she admitted. "I thought it might make our story less credible. The People regard nature as a force in itself. They take animal totems. Different animals mean different things. The raven is a trickster, possibly a shapeshifter. It's almost like the villain is telling us not to believe what we think...but people are too afraid to sort it out."

"And I didn't know what a raven's track might mean," Tiernan said. "I wonder what the investigators thought when they saw it. Or if they even paid it any mind. What did this Jacob assume was going to happen?"

"You'd have to ask him."

"And why was he blaming you?"

She didn't answer at first. Then she said, "For months before Mother moved us to Sioux Falls, bad things were happening on the rez. Stock dying, a man losing his mind, a house burning when no one was home. Always the incidents were somehow connected to the sign of the raven."

"But how does that involve *you?*"

"My father was a shaman. They blamed *him.*"

"Shaman...you mean like a holy man?"

"No, not holy. A *good* man who helps people. A spiritual leader."

"You said 'twas your mother who made you move... What about your da, then? Does he still live on the reservation?"

Ella went very still. "No," she said, her voice controlled. "He's dead."

The last thing she wanted to talk about with a near stranger. How had she let him lead her there? They were supposed to be talking about what happened the day before, not fifteen years before.

"Why am I thinking there's more to the story?" he asked.

For a moment, she resisted answering. But who else could she talk to? Certainly not the grandparents. She didn't want to worry them. And for some reason, she felt the need to tell Tiernan. What power did the man have over her?

Finally she said, "Because there *is* more. They thought Father was a sorcerer—evil—so they killed him."

"*Who* killed him?"

"The People who live on the rez. Nearly everyone. It was like they were in a fever, like their minds were affected and they couldn't stop themselves. Mother and I tried to make them stop. And Nathan and Leonard, two of his apprentices. But it was no use. They tied Father to a stake and set him on fire."

Shock registered in Tiernan's expression and he asked, "You saw it happen?"

She nodded and her hand shook as she lifted the mug to take another sip of beer. Not that it made her feel better. Nothing could.

"Most of it, anyway." Thankfully, Nathan had covered her eyes. "Father was not an evil man," she said. "The things that happened were caused by another, someone working in secret. Almost everyone believed my father was to blame. And then the whispers started—he was evil, he was a sorcerer, he needed to be destroyed."

"What did the authorities do? The tribal police?"

"Nothing. The incident was buried along with my father. Word leaked out and the FBI tried to investigate, but no one would talk."

"What about you and your family?"

"Mother and I could only tell them what we saw. We had no physical proof of anything. They couldn't bring an entire tribe to trial without there being political repercussions, so eventually the case just died." She met his intent gaze. "Now the superstition has already been resurrected, and I fear they will try to do the same to me as they did to Father."

Tiernan was silent for so long, her pulse began to thud. The green of his eyes seemed to deepen in color and the smile that usually hovered around his mouth was nowhere to be seen. He didn't seem put off by what she'd told him, rather he appeared to be angry.

"What made you come home, then?" he suddenly asked.

"I'm not home." She wondered that he didn't question her about why she feared she might be next to be thought evil. How could she not fear it when twice in two days the raven's track had appeared in her presence. "I'm simply a consultant for the movie."

"Is that the only reason you're here?"

"There are the grandparents—they're aging. Our People don't live long lives on the rez."

"But there is more," Tiernan said with certainty.

Ella flushed and hedged, "What more could there be?"

"Your wanting to resolve what happened to your da…even if you are reluctant to talk about it."

"It's been a long time. Fifteen years. I was a child then. And I'm no investigator."

"No," he said softly, "you're more. I sense it."

She started. "What do you mean…*more?*"

"I am not certain as to what exactly you can do…but you *are* your da's daughter."

"That's pretty obtuse."

Even so, her pulse picked up and she was having trouble again taking an easy breath.

Tiernan said, "You have some kind of power, Ella. I am aware of it in you every time I touch you."

"That's ridiculous."

"Is it?"

"What kind of power?" She could feel the speeding *tick-*

tick-tick of her pulse, and her voice rose in distress. "What would make you say such a thing?"

"If you don't want anyone else to know, I suggest you keep your voice down." He met her gaze and held it. "We are more alike than you know."

"Alike how?" Perturbed, Ella was beginning to regret agreeing to meet with Tiernan. She tried to turn the conversation on him. "Do you have some dark tragedy in your past you want to tell me about?"

"No, not in mine. I've seen to that," he said cryptically. "But I can sense things…know things that others don't."

A sense of relief passed through her and she tried to make light of it. "You mean, *fey* things like you were talking about yesterday?"

"Do not be too amused." Leaning close to her, he lowered his voice further, the serious timber cutting through her like a knife. "I can sense the rightness of things. And I can sense the presence of evil, which shadows the landscape here like a dark cloud at times. I read four-footed creatures and humans alike. If I open myself to it, their emotions cut through me…sometimes their thoughts." He sat back. "There's perhaps even more that I have not yet explored."

The way he told it put a shiver through her. Not that she was about to give him these supposed abilities. If he had them, she would have to stay away from him for sure. Her father's powers had gotten him killed and she didn't think she could stand to see that happen to anyone else.

Her voice challenging, she asked, "What *are* you?"

"I'm a McKenna," he returned simply. "The members of my family all have certain…gifts. Just as your da passed his powers on to you."

"I have no powers!" she snapped.

At least not anymore. There had been a time she'd been one

with the earth, in tune with the elements...able to make them shimmer and dance...but that was in the past...a past she had no intention of resurrecting.

Still, how could Tiernan know?

"You want to deny them because you think that will keep you safe," Tiernan said. "Gifts or powers are given to us for a reason. There's no denying them."

Ella didn't want to go there. She looked away from Tiernan. He was right, of course. Her father's powers had led to his death, so why would she want to follow in his footsteps? Perhaps she would feel more free to be herself—her father's daughter—if only she could figure out who had set him up.

Suddenly, Tiernan said, "If you agree, I can help you."

Startled by his sudden intensity, she asked, "Help me do what?"

"Find out what really happened to make people believe your da was evil. Perhaps why he died."

It was as if he could read her mind.

"I don't understand. Why would you want to do this?" she asked.

"I'm thinking there is a connection between the past and present—the raven's track. If that is so, then perhaps whoever was responsible for your da's death is also responsible for the death of Harold Walks Tall."

"But the authorities—"

"As it is," he went on, holding up a hand to stop her argument, "justice will never be done in Harold Walks Tall's name. Right now, the authorities are happy to pass off what is most likely murder as an accidental death. And you are correct—they would never consider the raven's track as evidence of anything. But 'tis not right for a man to pass unnoticed, without others being certain of why he died, of being able to mourn him properly."

Ella's heart was pounding now. She'd come back to the Black Hills under the pretense of work when she really wanted answers. Though she wasn't certain why she thought so, she felt as if Tiernan had some kind of investment in Harold Walks Tall's death and he was willing to help her get to the truth. She wouldn't have to act alone. Suddenly she felt as if a heavy burden were being lifted from her shoulders.

"Are you some kind of policeman or private investigator? Do you have a background for this kind of thing?" she asked.

"That I do not. But I have my McKenna gifts. And you have your da's powers if you will only free them. Together, we may be capable of anything."

A statement that made her take a big breath and press back the fear that threatened to swallow her whole.

TIERNAN WAITED PATIENTLY for Ella's answer. Once more, her fear came at him in waves. He could understand why she would be afraid to follow in her da's footsteps, afraid that there would be those who would watch her, expecting only evil from her. Who wouldn't be afraid to face death?

He wouldn't have suggested they investigate, but he didn't think they had a choice. One way or the other, Ella would be in danger. Better to face that danger head-on and cut it off before it got out of hand.

And perhaps if they found proof enough to convince the authorities of murder *this* time, 'twould make up for the last, when his aunt was written off.

Ella said, "I would like to know who was doing the things The People blamed Father for…the reason for his death. But *me* using some mysterious powers?" She shook her head as if that were impossible.

Tiernan didn't believe her, of course. She was in denial,

whether purposely or not. She didn't *want* to explore what to some was inexplicable. He had his own family secrets. Not all the McKennas were forthcoming about their psychic gifts—he wasn't forthcoming about the nightmare he'd lived since childhood—so he understood. Still, he also knew that, whether or not she wanted to believe it, the power would be there for her whenever she chose to call on it.

Whether or not she *would* choose to do so was another question.

"Then let us begin by using knowledge," he suggested, thinking the other could wait. "See if we can figure things out by talking it through."

"Don't you think I've thought on what happened for years? The person responsible for doing bad things on the rez had to be someone who corrupted spiritual powers."

"And that would be someone who had them, as well."

"I suppose."

"Was there another shaman competing with your da?"

"No, not that I ever heard. Father had three apprentices. Nathan was one of them. He and Leonard Hawkins tried to stop the crowd. The third apprentice was Jimmy Iron Horse." Her voice turned bitter on the last.

"It sounds as if you suspect this Jimmy."

She nodded. "He was with the crowd that horrible day. And now he's head of the tribal police, in a position of great power."

"And your cousin Nathan is connected to an organization of activists." He couldn't ignore the power he'd felt from Ella's cousin.

"I don't think he gets a salary from the organization," Ella said, "but he doesn't seem to be hurting for money."

Tiernan had noticed the gold buffalo hanging from Nathan's neck. That had been worth a pretty penny.

"What about the third man?"

"Grandmother told me Leonard Hawkins runs the casino and has the fanciest spread on the rez."

"So he has influence, as well," Tiernan mused. "Three men, three kinds of influence—military, political, financial. But what kinds of powers may they have learned from your da and how have they used them to get where they are?"

She cast her eyes down on the now-empty glass. "I—I'm not sure. Perhaps none of them was responsible."

Was Ella not sure or did she not want to implicate one of them? Tiernan wondered. Or was her hesitancy due to some other reason altogether?

Knowing it was likely one of the apprentices had manipulated the situation, wanting Ella to be comfortable with their approach, Tiernan asked, "So how do you suggest we start our investigation?"

"Talk to people, I guess."

"The men themselves?"

The suggestion made her pull away slightly. She took a breath and nodded. "I've been planning to talk to Nathan…but I suppose we need to talk to them all."

"Nathan first because he's your cousin?"

"He cared about Father," she said quickly. "Nathan tried to save him."

For Ella's sake, Tiernan hoped that was true and that Nathan hadn't simply been making a big show to take suspicion off himself. "What about the others? The casino manager?"

"Leonard. We could talk to him tonight, I suppose."

"Too late," Tiernan said. "I need to be up and on the set before dawn. Tomorrow, perhaps. We could head there right from the set."

"Okay."

"Ella, was one of the three more adept at shamanistic abilities than the others?"

"I'm not really sure, but Father always said Nathan worked the hardest."

Her growing discomfort was clear to Tiernan. He could not only feel it, he could see it in her expression, in her body language. Guilt at thinking it could be Nathan Lantero.

"You have a bond with him."

"He *is* my cousin."

"Is that the only reason?"

Her eyes told him she was fighting with an old emotional wound. "Nathan saved my life."

Ella absently rubbed at her left arm through the sleeve of her blouse. Tiernan wanted to ask her why, but something kept him from it, made him leave it to her to tell in her own time. He'd gotten enough from her for one night. He was, after all, still a stranger to her.

Not for long, though, Tiernan thought, feeling his gut clench and his throat tighten. It was clear to him that soon enough they would know each other in a way that most people couldn't even imagine, and while he knew he should avoid the situation—avoid her—he wasn't going to.

A slippery slope this, but Tiernan told himself he could handle it, he could be around the woman without invoking the family curse.

All he had to do was make sure he kept his distance and didn't fall in love with Ella Thunder.

Chapter Five

Tiernan had given her a lot to think about, and Ella was half distracted throughout the next morning as she worked with Jane Grant on set. Together, they watched the crew prepare for the Ghost Dance.

"After the opening prayers," Ella said, thinking of the real Ghost Dance, now more than a century old, "the participants joined hands and danced in a circle. The sick danced in hopes of being cured, and as the dance went on for hours, many of them fell unconscious or went into a trance."

Jane was taking notes. "We're planning on following Little Fawn, but other dancers could fall around her. I'll talk to Max about it," she said of the film's director Max Borland, who was working with his camera crew at the other end of the pasture. "It'll be up to him, of course."

Hoping the director was as concerned with the authentic details as Jane seemed to be, Ella continued, "Afterward, the dancers would sit in a circle and relate their experiences and visions."

They talked some more about the little details that could be added to the scene to make it more realistic. Then Jane said, "I'm going to go over the dance sequence with Max, see what he thinks. Why don't you take a break."

A little hungry since she'd left too early to get breakfast, Ella retreated to the large canopied area that served as the mess tent. There were a bunch of tables and food carts. She fetched herself a mug of coffee, a hard-boiled egg and a banana. A few crew members and more actors sat and studied scripts as they ate.

Ella spotted Bear Heart, a friend of Grandfather's who'd defied Lakota statistics to live into his mideighties. She didn't remember seeing him in the crowd that had demanded her father's death, so when he stood and waved her over to his table away from the others, she acquiesced.

"Ella Thunder, I would recognize you anywhere. You look like Joseph."

"Thank you. I am honored."

"Joseph would be proud of such a daughter, one who is educated and sees that The People are represented fairly and accurately in this movie."

"I'll do what I can," she promised. "What are you doing here?"

His grin split his leathered face. "Making my movie debut and becoming a matinee idol. Women will swoon when I dress in my feathers."

Ella laughed. "I'm sure they will."

Bear Heart picked up his tray. "Welcome home. You are needed."

Ella's laughter faded and she waited for him to say something about her following in her father's footsteps, but he simply stared at her a moment longer and nodded his satisfaction, then took his tray to the clearing station.

Ella claimed the table for herself. Peeling the shell from her egg, she couldn't help but wonder what Tiernan was doing right now.

With their agreement to investigate the deaths of her father and Harold Walks Tall, a delicate bond had been woven between them. Her only worry was Tiernan's belief that she had inherited her father's powers.

How had he even known about that? After Father's death, she'd buried anything she'd known about shamanistic abilities, so who would even guess what was possible? Surely Tiernan hadn't spoken to anyone about her.

"Ella, can I talk to you for a moment?"

Startled out of her thoughts about the man, Ella looked up to see Marisala Saldana, the young Lakota woman who was playing Little Fawn. In the film, her character would fall in love with one of the young soldiers and run away with him only to die for love.

Marisala slid into the seat opposite Ella. "I need a love potion."

Ella raised her eyebrows at this statement. The woman was breathtaking with naturally bronzed high cheekbones and full lips that would be the envy of any model. Marisala could no doubt get any man she chose just by blinking those amber eyes at him.

Why in the world did someone so beautiful think she needed the aid of magic?

"I don't do love potions," Ella said. "I don't do any potions at all."

"But I'm sick with love, Ella."

Marisala was as dramatic as only a young woman could be. Fifteen years ago, she'd been ten, a mere child, with nothing to do with Joseph Thunder's death, so Ella was comfortable being herself around the other woman.

"Are you saying there's a man with a pulse who isn't interested in you?"

"Oh, he's interested, but I want to bind him to me in a way no woman before ever has."

No doubt Marisala was hoping for marriage, Ella thought,

then wondered who the man might be. Lakota? Or someone from the cast and crew?

"That kind of commitment takes time, Marisala. It's something you need to work on, not rush."

Although she hadn't had a good example at home, Ella remembered. Marisala's father had left her mother high and dry, with no other family to turn to.

"I can pay," Marisala wheedled. "I'm not like the others. I have plenty of money."

Again Ella arched her eyebrows. Marisala's father left her and her mother penniless. She continued to live on the Bitter Creek Reservation, with no visible means of support before landing the role, but plenty of money? Hmm, maybe she was being paid more than Ella imagined.

"It's not a matter of money," Ella told her.

"Please, I'm desperate to get power over this man."

Ella frowned at the odd way Marisala phrased the request. Power? The idea made her uncomfortable.

"Nevertheless," Ella said, "there's nothing I can do for you."

"But you're a shaman. You're supposed to fix whatever is wrong with a person, aren't you?"

Ella sighed. "I'm not a shaman."

"That's not what The People say. They say you trained with your father from the time you were a child. That you have powers. Some even wonder if you're like him—evil—but *I* don't believe it."

Ella nearly choked on her coffee. Her heart began to thunder. People thought she was evil?

After seeing the raven's track and then connecting it to her, had Jacob gone back to the rez and started spreading nasty rumors?

"I'll tell you again. I'm not a shaman. I have no powers. I don't know how to make potions."

"If you don't know anything, then why are you acting as consultant for the spiritual scenes?"

The young woman's incensed tone made Ella lose her patience. Feeling as if she'd been cornered, Ella had to get away from Marisala. "I'm sorry, Marisala," she said, rising and taking her half-empty mug of coffee, "but I need to go consult. Now."

"Oh, all right. I'll leave you alone," Marisala called after her. "But if I can't figure out what else to do to solve my problem. I'll be back to get what I need. Or else. People shouldn't cross me—"

Ella cut her off. "Consider me warned."

What kind of a threat was that supposed to be? Marisala sounded as if she could be a little vindictive if she didn't get what she wanted, Ella thought as she went in search of Jane Grant. Marisala could spread rumors about her as easily as Jacob. Hopefully the threat was empty.

Approaching the Ghost Dance set, Ella spotted Jane with Max. Rather than being in conference as Jane had suggested would happen, the producer and director were sharing a close, personal moment. Jane's back was against a fence and Max Borland was so close a piece of paper wouldn't fit between them. The director was tall and powerfully built, his youthful-looking body in contrast with his leathery skin and silver buzz cut. He had to be twenty years older than Jane, but the age difference didn't seem to make any difference to either of them.

Wondering if they'd been a couple in Hollywood or had found each other out here in the wilds of South Dakota, Ella kept her distance and waited in a shady area set up with chairs. Perhaps their relationship gave Jane more power over what went on in the movie.

Forcing the encounter with Marisala from her mind, Ella purposely thought about Tiernan and his willingness to help her, a virtual stranger, delve into the past.

Like Marisala, Tiernan had talked about powers that she'd turned her back on fifteen years before. She wouldn't know how to call on them now. How did he know the potential was there? she wondered again. Perhaps Tiernan really was psychic, knowing things that a normal person wouldn't.

Which made him unsafe to be around, Ella thought, reminded of her father's fate.

If the wrong people decided he was doing something he shouldn't with his psychic abilities, Tiernan could be a danger to himself, and to her, as well.

Good reason not to get too close.

ALL DAY LONG, Tiernan thought about Ella anytime he wasn't dealing directly with the horses, which kept his mind occupied, so by the time they met at the parking lot, he was eager to see her. Too bad they didn't have a more positive reason for being together. Whenever he was around her, he had trouble thinking straight.

"Ready to go?" he asked.

He could not only sense her nerves, he could see them in her eyes, in the way she forced her lips into a smile. That she feared what she would learn might be natural, but her physical reactions made him suspect there was something deeper at work here.

Ella cleared her throat and asked, "Are you sure you really want to do this? If it was the beer talking last night, I'd understand."

"I wouldn't be letting the brew do my talking for me, sweet Ella. I am at your service," he said with a sweep of his broad-brimmed hat. "So 'tis to the casino, then?"

"Right. I called to make sure Leonard was there now. He's supposed to be working all night."

"Will you be riding with me?"

She nodded. "I caught a ride with Nathan this morning so

we wouldn't have two vehicles. I mean, I can walk home from the casino."

"Good thinking."

When they got to his truck, Tiernan opened the passenger door and tried to help Ella inside. She moved too fast for him and dodged his hand as though she couldn't bear for him to touch her. Frowning, he closed the door and circled the truck. He couldn't help feel some disappointment at Ella's cues—she obviously didn't want to get too close.

Perhaps that was for the best. He found her attractive—too attractive. It wasn't just her looks, but her struggle with who she really was. And her heart—big and brave. She was willing to face a scary past to get to the truth of what happened to her father.

Ella Thunder was the kind of lass a man could fall in love with, which for him, was unthinkable. He really should stay away from her.

He really should.

Starting the engine, he glanced at her. She seemed too deep in thoughts of her own to notice.

As he left the parking lot, he considered the complexity of why he really had agreed to help her. Yes, he thought Harold Walks Tall's killer deserved justice, but he didn't know the man any more than he knew Ella's da.

He was doing this for himself—as if it could make up with his failure to convince the *gardai* that his aunt had been murdered—and he was doing this for Ella.

There had to be a reason for the psychic connection he sensed every time he was near her—surely she felt it, as well. He had never experienced anything quite like that with another woman. There had to be a reason for it. Fate. Something he couldn't avoid.

Maybe the unexpected connection was the very reason that Ella had avoided him, however. Maybe that's why she'd looked so scared. He got it. Truly. But he couldn't stay away from her. Even knowing that he was asking for all kinds of trouble, Tiernan couldn't *not* try to help Ella—to protect the too-vulnerable lass—in any way he could.

"Anything I should know about this Hawkins lad before I meet him?" Tiernan asked.

Ella shrugged. "I don't know him as an adult. I haven't even seen him since I returned. I remember Leonard as being not so serious about becoming a shaman. He always came up with some excuse to get out of the work he didn't want to do. I know he exasperated Father at times. But he was still young—maybe twenty—and always charming in his apologies, always making promises to do better. Father never had the heart to send him away."

Leonard Hawkins sounded like the exact opposite of the ultra-serious Nathan Lantero, Tiernan thought.

The ride to the reservation wasn't long but it could take a man's breath away. The road wound through forested area, with dips and sharp curves but no guardrails. In places, the road switched back on itself sharply and the land quickly fell away. He imagined there had been more than one accident with someone driving too fast, especially in the dark or in foul weather.

At last they passed a sign saying they were entering Bitter Creek Reservation land. The road straightened and Tiernan tensed a little as he drove past sorry-looking houses and trailers that spoke to poverty. Ella guided him straight to the center of town and a plain single-story brick building. A gas station and auto repair sat to one side, and there was a small general store across the way. The casino was the biggest building on the rez as far as he could see—definitely bigger than the nearby government offices that housed the tribal council, tribal police and health center, among other services.

Tiernan parked his truck near the door and was out of the cab and at Ella's side by the time she opened her own door and slid from the passenger seat.

Again, she avoided his touching her.

"You'd better remove that," she said, indicating the sheathed knife at his waist. "Or they won't let you in."

He nodded and quickly removed it. "I've gotten used to wearing this since I came to South Dakota. I never know when I'll need it out in this wilderness."

He threw it on the truck floor and then slammed the door shut and followed Ella into the casino.

The moment he stepped inside, Tiernan had to catch his breath—a cloud of smoke hovered in the atmosphere, reminding him of Irish pubs before the ban on smoking had gone into effect five years ago. Never having been addicted to tobacco himself, he'd been glad of the change. Now he felt as if he could hardly breathe.

"We'll have to ask someone where to find Leonard," Ella said over the musical sound of dozens of slot machines, "then head for the cashier cage." Stopping suddenly, she pulled close to him and lowered her voice. "Uh-oh, the cashier doesn't look very friendly."

Tiernan noted the middle-aged Lakota woman who frowned as if she'd had a bad day. She was sorting a pile of chips.

"We can fix that." He stepped forward and gave the woman his best smile. "A pleasant evening to you, darlin'. If you would be so kind to point out Leonard Hawkins to me, I would be in your debt."

The woman's expression softened a bit. "Do you have an appointment with Mr. Hawkins?"

"No," he said, placing an arm around Ella's back and pushing her forward. "But this charming woman is an old friend of your employer. I'm sure he'll be happy to see her."

The woman eyed Ella with suspicion. "I don't know. He doesn't like surprises."

Tiernan wondered if good-looking women often surprised the casino manager at his place of work.

"I used to live on the rez when I was a kid," Ella said. "I'm back visiting relatives and thought I would catch up with some old friends."

"If I get in trouble—"

Tiernan interrupted. "Nah-nah, we will not be saying a word about who sent us in his direction."

The cashier considered it for a few seconds, then said, "I suppose there's no harm. He's in the office."

"And that would be where?"

The woman indicated the direction.

"Thank you, darlin'." Tiernan winked at her and moved off, Ella in tow.

"You certainly can turn on the charm when you want," she muttered.

Tiernan grinned. "Shall I be turning it on for you, then?"

"Don't bother, McKenna." She raised one eyebrow. "I have your number."

"Hmm, I shall have to do something about that, Thunder."

He laughed and then had to work to keep up with Ella as she sped up past a handful of gaming tables—poker, blackjack, roulette and craps—and led the way to the office. He spotted Nathan Lantero at one of the poker tables.

Nathan saw them, as well, and once more, Tiernan got a weird vibe from the man. The way Nathan was looking at him and Ella made Tiernan think he would be trouble.

Chapter Six

When they entered the office, no one was inside, but raised voices indicated an inner room behind one of the two doors on the rear wall.

"Ooh, sounds like someone is unhappy," Ella said. "Maybe we came at the wrong time. I suppose we should have made an appointment."

"Then you would have had to explain yourself and the man could have said no. This way you can simply say you wanted to stop by to see an old friend."

"That's stretching it a little, but okay," she said.

Listening intently, Tiernan heard a man say, "Don't ever make me warn you again or you'll regret it!"

Just then, the office door flung open and a man in dusty work clothes exited without closing the door behind him. He pushed by them rudely, knocking shoulders with Tiernan, who felt careening emotions from the brief touch.

Before he could sort them out, another man—Leonard Hawkins, no doubt—came to close the door. He was dressed in a well-tailored suit with a crisp white shirt and a designer silk tie. His hair had the look of a hundred-dollar cut, Tiernan thought. Not much of the Lakota to be seen beyond lightly bronzed skin and fathomless dark eyes. He was handsome enough, but at the moment, his chiseled face was twisted with irritation.

When the man realized he wasn't alone, he took a step back and tried to cover, immediately forcing a smile. "Are you looking for me?"

"Leonard…it's Ella."

"Ella?" Leonard started. "Little Ella Thunder?"

"Not so little anymore."

Tiernan watched the other man transform himself from an angry casino manager to a welcoming friend. Leonard put his arms around Ella and hugged her, then with hands on her shoulders held her away from him to take every inch of her in with those penetrating eyes.

Tiernan twitched but held himself in check.

"I always knew you were going to grow into a beauty," Leonard said.

Ella's color rose and a smile stretched her lips. Tiernan wasn't smiling—the man was too smooth, and there was something off about him.

"What are you doing here?" Leonard asked. "How long is this visit?"

While the questions sounded friendly enough, Tiernan sensed Leonard was a little too anxious for the answers. His emotions didn't fit with his expression.

Why would he care what Ella was doing on the rez or how long she was going to stay?

"I'm acting as consultant on the movie. It gives me a chance to visit with Grandmother and Grandfather. I expect I'll be here for two or three weeks."

"Well…time enough for us to catch up. Good. Good." Finally Leonard looked to Tiernan. "And who is this? Husband? Significant other?"

"Friend." Wanting to make physical contact—better to read

the man—Tiernan held out his hand. "Tiernan McKenna, horse wrangler for the duration of the film."

Leonard shook. "Well, nice to meet a friend of Ella's." Then he narrowed his gaze on Tiernan. "You're not from around these parts, though. Your accent—?"

"Ireland." The skin at the back of Tiernan's neck crawled and he focused in on the other man.

Ella said, "Tiernan's visiting relatives in the area, too. The MKF Ranch."

Leonard pulled his hand from Tiernan's. "I know it—your family also owns the refuge."

They'd only made contact for a few seconds, but it was enough for Tiernan to surmise the man wasn't as happy to see them as he made out. Why? Because Ella wasn't alone? Or was it Ella's presence that made the man cautious?

"Why are we standing here? Let's go get you something to eat. Dinner's on me."

"You don't have to do that, Leonard."

"If the guy in charge can't even treat his own friends, then what good's having the job?"

As they left the office, Tiernan glanced over to the poker tables. Nathan had already left.

Dinner was an all-you-can-eat buffet with slabs of prime rib. The restaurant area tucked into one corner of the casino was modest in size and therefore crowded. Leonard took them past the line and got them a table immediately.

Was he trying to impress Ella or to keep her at bay? Tiernan wondered. It *would* be easier to avoid any tough subjects in a crowd, if that was Leonard's intention.

Leonard called over a waitress. "What would you like? Champagne? A cocktail?"

"Iced tea," Ella said.

Tiernan nodded. "I'll take the same."

Leonard shrugged. “Make it three.” When the waitress left, he said, “If you change your mind about that drink, don’t be shy.”

He then herded them to the buffet.

They returned to the table, plates groaning with food. Small talk got them through the meal. Tiernan began to wonder if Ella would ever get to the real reason they were there.

It was only after the waitress refilled their iced teas and they sat back in the booth and pushed their plates away that Ella said, “Leonard, I’m really surprised that you turned to something as commercial as a casino as your life’s work. Well, considering you were heading in the opposite direction when you apprenticed with my father.”

“I loved Joseph—the only reason I wanted to work with him. Truthfully, I’m not sure I would have made a good shaman. Flighty—that’s what Joseph used to call me. He was right. I always did like to have a good time. I still do.” Leonard heaved a sigh. “And then there’s what happened to your father. Nothing has been the same since he’s been gone. Fear drove me away from even considering a spiritual life.”

Tiernan didn’t get fear off Leonard. He didn’t get much at all, which was curious. Unless Leonard was somehow blocking him. Or did Leonard think he was blocking Ella?

“A casino is as far away from a spiritual vocation as you can get,” Tiernan observed.

“True, but I still wanted to do good for The People. The rez needed an influx of money. A casino was the logical way of getting it, so I worked the tribal counsel to get approval,” Leonard said smoothly. “And they commissioned me to see that it was done. Once this place was built, I was, of course, the logical choice to run it.”

“Of course,” Ella said.

No of course about it, Tiernan thought. The man was self-aggrandizing and Ella didn't seem to realize it. She was taking Leonard at his word. And she wasn't asking him about the past, the reason they'd come here.

Thinking to correct that, Tiernan said, "Ella has told me that you tried to save her da."

"A futile effort. The whole rez turned against poor Joseph. Everyone but Nathan and me. And his family, of course."

"Because someone made it seem like Joseph Thunder was an evil man."

Leonard looked from Tiernan to Ella. "You think someone set up your father for some reason?"

"How else can you explain the bad things that happened, seemingly without cause?" Ella asked. "Horses getting sick, the fire, Nelson Bird losing his mind…"

"All things that could have happened without *anyone's* help. The Lakota are sometimes too superstitious. When things went wrong, everyone jumped to the wrong conclusion about Joseph. It was like a fever that spread through the rez."

"I remember," Ella whispered.

For a moment, Tiernan felt what it had been like to be a young girl panicked at the idea of losing her da. Ella's terror welled up in his body…her determination to save him focused his mind…and then heat spreading up his left arm jerked him back to the present.

What the hell?

"The thing is, Leonard, I was too young to know what was really going on. My parents sheltered me, and when the rumors started, they cut me off from everyone. I think they feared for me. But you were an adult—"

"A matter of opinion," Leonard said, laughing.

Ella didn't lose a beat. "So I was hoping that you might be able to give me details about anything that was off."

"To tell the truth, I've put that time out of mind."

"Then think on it. It's important to me. Father's death has haunted me for fifteen years."

"It's time to let go, don't you think?"

"Only when I know the truth."

"You already do, Ella. You just don't want to accept it. You don't want it to be a rush of bad luck and superstition that escalated. You want to place blame."

A silent Tiernan tried to tap into the man, but he remained blocked.

Ella said, "I just want the truth…whatever it is…and one way or another, I intend to get to it."

"One way or another?" Leonard stared hard at her. "What does that mean?"

"Just what it sounds like."

"You always did obsess on things when you were a kid. I guess you haven't changed."

"People rarely change," Tiernan broke in, unwilling to be left out of the conversation any longer. "Undoubtedly you are still the same person you were fifteen years ago. You just wear a different skin."

A skin he couldn't penetrate, not even when Leonard seemed to relax as he laughed.

"No doubt that's true."

"And then there's the person responsible for the bad things happening on the reservation," Tiernan said. "I understand he used a raven's track to mark his work then…and he's still doing it now."

Leonard went still and silent for a moment, then in a tight voice asked, "What does that mean?"

Ella said, "There was a raven's track in the ground where Harold Walks Tall fell to his death."

"So you think…what?"

"That the poor lad was murdered, of course," Tiernan said, watching for the other man's reaction.

Leonard checked his watch and then shot to his feet. "I hate to do this, but I have to leave. You two can sit here as long as you like. Order anything you want. It's all on me."

"I couldn't eat another bite," Ella said, also standing.

Leonard gave her a quick hug. "Great to see you, Ella. Maybe we can get together again before you go back to your life."

Ella was smiling. "That would be great. As would your thinking about what might have happened—"

"Got it." Leonard saluted. "If I remember something, I promise I'll let you know."

"I can use all the help I can get."

Leonard was already hurrying off.

Sensing her disappointment in not getting more from the meeting, Tiernan said, "Too bad he wasn't more open."

She shrugged. "I think he was as open as he could be. He's the first one we talked to. I have to admit I should have done this long ago—reconnect with old friends."

"He's one of the suspects," Tiernan reminded her.

Ella didn't say anything.

Tiernan couldn't leave it at that. "There was something off about Leonard Hawkins. He puts on a grand act."

"Is that your McKenna *fey*-side making a judgment call?" she asked.

Hearing the annoyance in her tone, Tiernan backed off and wondered if she could really be objective about any of the people who'd been in her old life.

If not, he wasn't certain they would ever identify the villain.

ELLA THUNDER WAS trouble.

He should have known she wouldn't be content to do the

consulting job she'd been hired to do and mind her own business. He should have known she wouldn't let go of the past.

Darting her and then leaving her be had been a mistake, one he wouldn't make again. He should have sent her over the cliff to join Harold Walks Tall. Then he would have been done with her for good.

While he'd been able to leave the scene of the murder without her spotting him, she obviously wasn't content with getting off with her life. Wasn't content with Harold's death being declared accidental. Wasn't content with the fifteen-year-old cover-up.

Ella Thunder was sticking her nose where it didn't belong.

Just like her father, Joseph, had.

And just like her father, he would see her dead before she could expose him.

Chapter Seven

Ella had loosened her hair from the ponytail and was running a comb through it when two women entered the ladies' room—Ami Badeau and her mother, Hannah. Ella recognized the sour-faced younger woman immediately. Ami had been the one who'd pushed her out of the way when she'd tried to get to her father.

Clenching her jaw, Ella tried to get her hair back in its clip, but her hands shook so, it flew from her fingers.

"Here, let me help," Hannah said, picking up the clip and handing it over.

"Thank you," Ella murmured. Not knowing whether Hannah had been part of the crowd, she was unable to meet the woman's eyes.

"Mother, what are you doing…touching *her!*"

"Ami! Mind your manners!"

"I'm simply trying to protect you."

"Stop listening to that crazy Jacob!"

Ami already had her arm around her mother's shoulders and was turning the woman away. Setting the clip in place, Ella grabbed her bag and rushed out of the restroom. She was shaking inside, wanting in the worst way to be out of the casino *now.* Unfortunately, Tiernan was nowhere to be seen.

Ella was gazing around, looking for him, wondering if a slot machine had seduced him, when a broad-built man in a black tribal police uniform stopped directly in front of her.

"Ella Thunder, you cause any trouble and I'm going to lock you right up."

Under attack for the second time in mere minutes, Ella started. She narrowed her gaze at the man whose buzz-cut hair topped a craggy face. Though she didn't recognize him at first, the eyes did it for her. She'd always been spooked by the pale gray eyes in Jimmy Iron Horse's otherwise distinctively Lakota face, his only testament to mixed blood on both sides of his family.

"Jimmy, good to see you, too," she said stiffly. She reminded herself that he was the only one of Father's apprentices who'd gone with the crowd rather than trying to stop her father's murder. And therefore suspect himself. "Trouble how?"

"Jacob told me about seeing the raven's track—"

"Which I didn't do!" Had he told everyone on the rez? she wondered.

"So you say."

"Jacob is an overly superstitious man. Believe sorcery is at work if you want, Jimmy, but I wasn't the one who left the sign on the fence post. Besides, nothing bad has happened to the horses."

"Yet," he said, his spooky gray eyes boring into her.

"Is there a problem here?" came Tiernan's welcome voice from behind her.

He slipped an arm around her waist and held her fast to his side. A shiver of something clandestine between them swept through her.

Focusing, she said, "Apparently not yet."

"Not that anyone has proved," Jimmy qualified.

"What the heck does that mean?"

"I know about Harold Walks Tall." Jimmy's gaze shifted to Tiernan. "You the one with her?"

"Aye, we found the body together."

"You ought to stay away from trouble, especially here on the rez. Ella takes after her old man, which means she's dangerous to be around."

"How dare you?" Now she was getting angry.

"Experience," Jimmy said. "One I don't want to see repeated. My duty is to protect the tribe and the rez and remove unwanted influences."

"I am *part* of the tribe," Ella reminded him. "And I'm not going anywhere until I'm good and ready."

"That might be sooner than you think," he said, smirking as he walked away.

"What does *that* mean?" she shouted after him, but Jimmy didn't so much as slow his stride.

Other people were staring at her, though. People who'd ushered her father to his death? Did they know who she was? Ella began to shake inside.

Tiernan gave her a gentle squeeze. "I think we should be getting away from here."

"I think you're right."

They headed out of the casino into the dark and straight to Tiernan's truck. He unlocked the door for her, then stopped her from getting in.

"Wait. Something is wrong."

He reached inside and pulled out a flashlight. Shining the light on the front tire showed it to be flat, shredded strands of rubber decorating the pavement. He cursed softly, then went around the truck, checking each wheel.

"All four," he said. "Someone slashed all four tires."

"*What?* Who would do that?" Guilt slid through her. "It's

because you're with me. It has to be. Someone is taking his dislike for me out on you."

"Or trying to warn me away from asking too many questions."

"Leonard wouldn't do this."

"I didn't say he did. Though we didn't ask questions of anyone else."

"More likely, it was Jimmy." Ella couldn't see an officer of the law doing something so destructive, but who else? "That's why he was gloating when he walked away. We should report this…but to whom? If Jimmy did do it, reporting it would be futile since he's the head of the tribal police. He'd probably tell everyone that I put some kind of curse on your truck."

Tiernan swept the light over the ground around the car. "Look at this," he said, stopping the flood of light near one of the tires.

Ella gasped. A raven's track. "Our telling anyone about it will only make people take a closer look at me. They'll think I did it myself."

Tiernan smudged the scratching with his foot until it disappeared. "Let's go over to the petrol station, see what they can do for us."

Ella's pulse rushed through her as she walked with him. What did the sign and the slashed tires mean? Was it simply a warning to leave the rez? Or something more?

At the gas station, she stopped at the door. "I'll wait outside for you."

So she could think.

Part of her wanted to run back to Sioux Falls, but the other part was angry. Not about to be scared away, Ella closed her eyes and thought of her father and his strength in the face of terror. She could see him as he was that last day before fire tore at his flesh.

I will not let anyone drive me away, Father.

You are brave, Ella.

I'm frightened. I don't know if I can do this.

You can do anything you choose. You learned well, daughter. Now you must use what you know. Use your mind the way I taught you.

It has been too long.

It is time.

"They can't do anything—not tonight."

Tiernan's voice jerked Ella back to the situation.

"The lad told me to come back in the morning when someone could get me a price on new tires and then have someone go fetch them from Custer."

"I'm really sorry—"

"'Tis not your fault."

"In a way it is. If I hadn't involved you, this wouldn't have happened."

"I volunteered, remember."

Tiernan gave her a blinding smile that made her heart skip a beat. This time, she fought the invisible link that threatened to bind her to him.

"After what happened," she said, "I'm not holding you to anything." Who knew how far the culprit would go next?

"Something as inconsequential as ruined tires is not going to change my mind."

"What if it's more?"

"We will take things as they go. As my grandmother always says, 'Do not be lookin' for trouble, Tiernan, lad, for trouble is sure ta find ye soon enough.'"

Ella smiled. "All right."

Tiernan's expression said he wanted to tell her something more, then shifted into neutral. "I guess I should be walking, then."

"I'll drive you, of course." She caught his wrist and tugged on it. "The house is this way."

Flushing with inexplicable feelings, she let go of him. They walked in silence, giving her time to wonder why they seemed linked together. What was it that had brought them together in the first place? And why did she feel like a battery that was plugged in and charging every time he was near her?

They arrived at the house without her having the answer. "Here we are."

"No lights on to welcome you home?"

"The grandparents go to bed early. Electricity is one expense they can limit. Besides, I'm used to finding my way through the place. This used to be our house," she admitted. "I don't have to go in. I have the keys on me."

Pulling them from her purse, she jingled them at him and then unlocked the SUV.

Within minutes they were back on the winding road cutting first across reservation land, which soon gave way to refuge land. Ella wasn't fond of driving this road with its dips and drop-offs and hairpin curves during the day. At night the road could be treacherous, so she took it slower than normal. Undoubtedly the reason another set of lights in her rearview mirror approached so fast. The driver put on his brights and flicked them several times.

"Oh, great, this guy is in a big hurry."

Tiernan glanced back. "Isn't he getting a little too close?"

"For my comfort, yeah, but he'll get tired of waiting for me to speed up and will just go around us."

Only he didn't.

The brights in her mirrors nearly blinded her. She couldn't make out anything other than the vehicle was a dark, old model truck. It stayed directly behind them so close that Ella felt as if it was right in her trunk.

And then it was.

The first time it was a tap.

"Hey!"

And then the tap became a bump, making Ella speed up whether or not she wanted to.

"What the hell does he think he's doing?" Tiernan muttered, now turning in his seat as far as the seat belt would let him. "'Tis impossible to see anything beyond the brights."

But Ella could see that no matter how fast she went, the truck behind was staying glued to her rear, trying to make her go faster.

The SUV veered toward the drop-off, the tires spewing gravel from the side of the road. The breath caught in Ella's throat and she jerked the wheel so the SUV careened away from the edge to the other side of the road. An oncoming car made her jerk the other way to correct. The SUV swayed and went up on two wheels and then back down to four with a hard thunk.

"We're going too fast!" If she didn't slow down, they could capsize or go over the embankment. She looked up into the rearview mirror and saw the lights approaching from behind again. "I can't control it."

"Calm down, darlin', 'tis a fine job of driving you're doing. 'Tis only your nerves making you think you can't control the vehicle."

As Tiernan spoke, he placed a calming hand on her shoulder. The effect rippled through her until at last, she breathed easier.

"What did you do to me?"

"Convinced you of my confidence is all."

But how? What magic did he use on her?

She didn't ask, rather aimed her full concentration on getting them safely to flat land. Able to see the full road and any oncoming vehicles ahead, she straddled the line and halfway through the next curve sped up, finally putting some distance between them and the truck.

Though she was barely familiar with the road, she remembered that at the end of this hilly stretch there was a straight run across a flat piece of land that went on half a mile. They were almost there.

"Hang on, I'm going to get a look at whoever is trying to run us off the road."

"What are you planning on doing?"

"Just watch."

A couple hundred yards into the flat, she slowed and put the SUV into four-wheel drive, then circled onto unpaved road. She clicked on her brights just in time to get a good look at the side of the truck as it passed them and sped on.

"Do you recognize it?" Tiernan asked.

Sick inside, she nodded. "Nathan's truck."

"How can you be certain?"

"I just rode in it this morning."

"Let's get out of here," Tiernan said. "And keep a watch out in case he comes back."

Ella's nerves were on edge again the entire five minutes it took them to get to refuge headquarters. She didn't relish the drive back and decided she would take the long way around. No more shortcuts for her.

Stopping near the front door, she said, "I guess I should report this…for all the good it will do."

"You're not going back to the reservation alone." He touched her and said, "You're shaking. Come inside and have a cuppa."

"I shouldn't."

"I'm thinking you should. Now, come inside, Ella, and let me take care of you."

Being taken care of sounded great right now. Relieved that

she didn't have to be alone for a while, she scrambled out of the vehicle and let Tiernan take her in his arms for a moment. She shuddered and then surrendered to the cocoon of warmth and the deeper connection she felt with him.

"That's it," Tiernan murmured into her hair. "Relax."

The stress she'd felt on the chase had vanished only to be replaced by another kind of tension. Her pulse skittered through her and her skin grew hot and taut. She looked up at Tiernan. His expression was so serious, his gaze so deep, that she lost herself for a moment and rose on tiptoe to brush his lips with hers.

Tiernan held her tight and stared straight into her eyes. "What is it you want, Ella?"

Feeling as if all the air was suddenly squeezed out of her, thinking he was willing to give her whatever she did want, Ella said, "Just to thank you."

"Is that all? Truly?"

She blinked and wet her lips. "I—I don't know." This was crazy. She shouldn't be in his arms.

"'Tis honest. I don't know, either, lass. Shall we table this discussion to another time, then?"

Breathless, Ella nodded and Tiernan released her. Still, he took her hand and led her inside. His grip was warm and comforting, and despite her reservations, she was glad for the contact.

The reception room was dark until Tiernan switched on a light. "There you go."

"Are your relatives asleep this early?"

"Relax," he said. "I didn't notice Kate's SUV out there, so I assume they went out for the evening. Come sit in the kitchen. I'll put the kettle on to boil."

"As much as I hate having to do this, I need to call in the incident," she admitted. "The question is to whom? It was

Nathan, but we were on refuge land. Then again, local law enforcement would probably have to turn him back over to the tribal police. So I guess I have the answer."

"The phone is over there," he said, indicating one on the wall.

Reluctantly, Ella called tribal headquarters and said she needed to make an official report. The assistant put her through to Ted Grey. She was thankful to get someone she knew other than Jimmy, but not so thankful as to what the officer had to say.

"So you weren't hurt and your car wasn't actually damaged?" Ted questioned.

"No, but the driver was trying to cause an accident. I almost slid over the embankment. And I saw the vehicle—a truck—and know the owner." She took a deep breath and said, "Nathan Lantero."

"Isn't Nathan your cousin?" Ted asked, his voice suddenly thick with suspicion. "If it's a family matter, I don't know why you're bothering us."

"Because he tried to run me off the road!"

As she said it, Tiernan turned from the kettle on the stove and tuned in to her. That she could feel it put her off her game for a moment.

Ted asked, "You said this near-accident *just* took place?" He sounded as if he didn't really believe her.

"Like ten minutes ago."

"Then the driver couldn't have been Nathan."

"Why not?" Were Ted and Nathan buddies? she wondered, her grip on the phone tightening. She matched looks with Tiernan as she asked, "Is Nathan locked up?"

"Nope, but he was here an hour ago, making out a report—stolen truck. So it couldn't have been him."

Taken by surprise, Ella was speechless for a moment. If the truck really had been stolen, that meant Nathan hadn't tried to harm or at least to scare her. It hadn't been her cousin who'd tried running her off the road.

A bit relieved, she found her voice. "Are you looking for the truck?"

"Actively? Nope," Ted admitted. "But a description already went out. If anyone sees it and we are able to make an arrest, I'll get back to you."

Frustrated, she slammed the phone into its cradle.

"So…Nathan…?" Dropping tea bags into two mugs, Tiernan let the name dangle.

"Reported the truck stolen an hour ago."

"Stolen? And you believe that?"

"I want to. When I was a kid, Nathan was like a big brother to me. He saved my life. I don't want to think he changed into a bad person."

Or that he'd been a bad person all along, which, of course, was a distinct possibility.

The kettle began to whistle, so Tiernan filled the mugs with hot water. Then he handed her one.

"Give it a moment."

Taking it, she set it on the table. Her mind was whirling. "Maybe I should have told Ted about the slashed tires." Truthfully, she'd forgotten about them until just now. "So, do you think whoever slashed them was counting on my giving you a ride home?"

"A possibility, I would say."

"Then we were both targets. Someone is trying to scare us both away."

"Or worse."

"Or worse," she echoed. "But why would anyone want to hurt us?"

"Because we know too much?"

"What is it we know? Nothing!"

Frustrated anew, Ella picked up her mug and sipped at her tea. She didn't have long to think before hearing a vehicle pull up near the house. She looked to Tiernan.

"Kate and Chase are home." He set down his mug. "I'm going to tell them what happened. I'm sure Kate will want you to stay here for the night until we can think on what to do."

Ella had no argument for that.

But when Tiernan's cousin came in the door, followed by her husband—a tall man dressed in black jeans and a black shirt buttoned to the neck—he didn't have the opportunity to tell them anything.

"We have a problem," Kate immediately announced.

"What kind of problem?" Tiernan asked.

"Sick horses."

"Where?"

"The pasture at the set," Chase said.

"Is that where you've been?"

"Right. Nathan called to warn us."

"Nathan?" Ella repeated, feeling the air leave her lungs again. What did her cousin have to do with this?

Chase nodded. "He went to check on his horses and noticed several of ours had a rough cough and a clear discharge from the nose and eyes."

"I checked them out myself," Kate said. "They had swollen lymph nodes under their jaws. Looks like equine flu. They'll need extra care for at least a week."

Tiernan said, "We need to get them out of there before the rest of the herd becomes infected."

"Already done," Chase said. "Not that it's any guarantee that more won't get sick. The affected horses are in a corral near the barn. Let's just hope this is it, that there aren't more."

Though she wasn't a horse expert, Ella knew that equine flu could be a serious problem.

"We took Maggie over to the ranch. Mom is taking care of her," Kate said. "Then we came back here to get you. I figure it's going to be a long night. I can't believe this is happening right before the big party for Quin and Luz."

"An engagement party," Tiernan told Ella. "Kate's youngest brother is getting married, and there is going to be a big celebration tomorrow night at the ranch."

As the others discussed treatments and precautionary measures, Ella tried to think of something happy—the engaged couple's upcoming nuptials—but couldn't keep a terrible memory out of mind. Picturing a raven's track scratched on the post between refuge and rez pastures on the set, she could almost hear Jacob railing against her.

She felt nauseous.

This was the way her father's downfall had begun all those years ago....

Hot bile filled Ella's throat as she remembered how quickly the accusations surrounding Father had spread and escalated and wondered if fate had the same in store for her.

Chapter Eight

Tiernan suggested Ella stay at the house and try to get some sleep, but she insisted on accompanying him and Kate and Chase to the barn to help with the horses. Five of them were sick. So far. He'd seen influenza spread through a herd like wildfire, and he wouldn't bet there wouldn't be more equine victims by morning.

Being a veterinarian put Kate in charge. Even her husband deferred to her as she issued instructions on what she needed them to do for the horses.

"I want them in the barn, but let's get the floors hosed down and fresh hay put in the stalls first," she said.

From past experience with equine flu in Ireland, Tiernan knew they needed to keep the barn dust free and well ventilated. They all got busy, Ella working side by side with him. Apparently she knew her way around horses and wasn't afraid to put herself out.

A half hour later, the stalls were ready for their occupants.

"Make sure you clean your hands before touching any horse," Kate said.

She started with the horse she brought inside, taking a nasal swab and a blood sample, then checking the horse's temperature.

"How bad?" Chase asked.

"Only 100."

Odd that the horse should be so symptomatic, then, Tiernan thought. Usually a horse with flu had a temperature between 103 and 106 degrees. Kate took samples and temperatures from each of the horses. When none showed the expected high fever, she grew thoughtful, ran her hand through the nearest horse's mane and pressed her forehead into his cheek as if she were trying to read him.

"What?" Tiernan asked softly, knowing that Kate had a psychic bond to horses just as he did.

"I don't know. I don't see anything…nor sense anything. I simply have a weird feeling is all."

Ella frowned at them but didn't say anything as Tiernan narrowed his focus and concentrated on the nearest horse himself. He got nothing for his trouble.

"What do we do now?" Ella asked.

"Give them rest so they don't pick up any secondary infections," Tiernan told her.

Kate added, "I need to be sure of what's going on before deciding whether to give steroids to the pregnant mare. In the morning, I'll run the blood and nasal samples to the lab to see exactly what we have."

"Or don't have," Chase said.

Did Chase think the horses weren't really sick? Tiernan wondered. If not, they were great actors if the hoarse coughs were any indication. As the humans left the barn, a couple of the horses were hacking away.

As they headed for the house, Tiernan looked to Kate and Chase. "I meant to tell the two of you, Ella and I had some trouble of our own tonight. Vehicle trouble."

"So that's why when we drove in from the ranch, I didn't see the refuge truck," Chase said.

"I am sorry to be telling you all four tires were slashed outside the casino." Feeling guilty, he assured them, "Don't worry, I'll pay for them myself."

"That's not an issue," Chase said. "But what the hell's going on, Tiernan?"

"Nothing good. There is more." He tensed as he remembered the harrowing ride from the reservation to the refuge. "Ella gave me a ride back here and we're lucky we made it in one piece—someone tried running us off the road. 'Twas Nathan Lantero's truck, but he apparently reported it stolen the hour before."

As they entered the house, Chase kicked back his hat and frowned. "I don't like the sound of this. Who did you hack off and why?"

"Possibly a murderer," Ella said.

"The track of a raven was left where the man was found dead yesterday…the same marking connected with Ella's da, who was murdered by his own people fifteen years ago."

"You're *that* Thunder?" Kate sank into a chair in the reception area. "I remember hearing something about the shaman being killed… Oh, I'm so sorry."

"Thank you." Ella sat on the couch opposite.

"The authorities think Harold Walks Tall had an accidental fall, and we do not agree," Tiernan explained, sitting next to Ella but keeping a slight distance so she wouldn't distract him. "We're doing some investigating on our own."

"And whoever is responsible is trying to discourage you. I can't believe it's Nathan Lantero." Across the room in the work area, Chase wedged a hip on the desk. "I've known him too many years to believe something like this of him. He used to work for me."

"He worked for the refuge *before* he became an activist," Ella said. "I don't like thinking bad things about him, either.

I mean, he *is* my cousin and he did save my life once." Looking as if she had a rock in her stomach at the thought of Nathan's being guilty, Ella shook her head. "So I hope you're right, that it can't be Nathan."

Tiernan wasn't so certain. Nathan had been in the casino, but by the time they'd left Leonard's office, Nathan had vanished. Enough time for him to mess with the truck and plan how to scare the hell out of his cousin.

"I hope you and Chase don't mind," he said to Kate, "but I want Ella to stay here tonight. Her driving to the reservation alone isn't safe."

"Of course," Kate said. "Though it won't be any safer in the morning. Do you have someplace else you can stay?"

"No, not really."

Kate looked to her husband.

"She can stay as long as she needs to," Chase said. "We can scare up a cot—"

"Which I shall take," Tiernan said. "I will sleep on the back porch and Ella can have my room."

"No," Ella said. "I'll take the cot."

"Don't be arguing with me, Thunder. I shall win in the end. I always do."

In the end, Ella caved like he knew she would. She was tired, scared and obviously glad to have someone make decisions for her, if only for now.

As if *now* was long enough....

The more Tiernan got involved with Ella Thunder, the more certain he was that there was more waiting for them. He could fall for her if he let himself...if the prophecy of doom didn't hang over his head.

He would like nothing more than to sleep with the woman, to hold her close, to make love to her.

Which would put her in mortal danger.

Tiernan told himself to back off, to think of her as the sister he never had. Unfortunately, he'd never been good at taking orders, not even from himself.

When he threw himself on the cot to sleep, it was with her image in mind. The moment he scrunched his pillow beneath his cheek—exhausted and stressed—Tiernan felt the present slip away....

"C'mon, boy," she says, her voice shaking, "let us get out of here, quick now."

"What's wrong, Aunt Megan?" he asks, looking in the direction that she does and seeing a long, dark auto coming toward them.

"That man," she gasps, holding his hand tight and practically dragging him across the street, "he lost his son in a bombing and thinks my brothers are to blame!"

The scream of tires fills his ears and he looks back and trips.

And then she's screaming and lifting him by his arm so that it nearly pulls free of his shoulder and the next thing he knows he's flying through the air and then his ears fill with an explosion of sound....

AT DAYBREAK THE next morning, Ella called her grandparents and lied to them. Sort of. She said car trouble had kept her at a friend's house for the night, but she didn't elaborate. She figured she'd avoid telling them what had really happened so that they wouldn't worry. They'd already lost their son tragically and were too old and frail to deal with another frightening situation.

Which was the only reason she would be staying on the refuge—to protect them. Ella feared that if she remained in the house, danger would seek her there. Still, she had to make sure the grandparents were all right and figure out a way to break the news to them without giving Grandfather a heart attack.

After running Tiernan to the gas station for new tires, which she figured would take him a while since the station wasn't yet open, Ella drove home to change clothes and pack a case.

And there got a breathtaking surprise.

Nathan's truck was sitting outside the house.

Her pulse rushing through her, she ran to the house and threw open the door only to hear the clatter of breakfast dishes and Grandfather's laugh.

"Let me help you with those dishes," she heard Nathan say.

And then Grandmother said, "Just take your coffee and go in the other room, Nathan. I don't need help in my kitchen."

"All right."

Ella was still standing in the doorway when Nathan strolled into the living room, coffee mug in hand.

"Ella, there you are."

Still unsettled by his appearance—and by the appearance of his truck—Ella asked, "Nathan, what are you doing here?"

"Visiting the grandparents—they are my grandparents, too, remember. Do you have a problem with that?"

"No, not with that."

"What, then?" Nathan sauntered into the living room where he took a seat on the couch.

Ella followed but remained standing. "You reported your truck stolen yesterday."

"Someone *did* steal it."

"Then why is it parked outside?"

"Apparently, whoever took it left it near the government building sometime during the night. Jimmy Iron Horse called me about it a couple of hours ago. What the hell, Ella?" Nathan's expression darkened, sending a chill through her. "He also told me you claimed I tried running you off the road!"

"Did you?" she choked out.

"First, how could you think I would? Second, how could I when my truck was gone?"

A convenient story, Ella thought, clenching her jaw so she wouldn't say it. Nathan could be telling the truth. She'd thought Jimmy was the likeliest suspect when it came to framing her father. Maybe the head of the tribal police *was* the one who took the truck and then returned it.

"If I misjudged you, then I'm sorry for that." If Nathan indeed was innocent, Ella regretted thinking otherwise. "I need to get ready for work."

"Not until we talk. That's really why I stopped by this morning."

"Talk about what?"

"I saw you and McKenna with Leonard last night and wondered what was going on."

"I was catching up with an old friend."

"Is that all?"

"What else?"

"I don't know, Ella. Just be careful of Leonard. He's not exactly what he seems to be. He goes around talking like he's helping the rez by running the casino when all he's really helping is himself."

"I don't understand. He's given people work, the tribe money."

"Not so much. Unfortunately, the casino simply isn't making the profit it should be." Nathan took a last sip of coffee, then set the mug down on a table. He seemed both concerned and angry as he said, "The rez is little better off than it was before the casino was built."

"Then how did Leonard get enough money for his fancy house?"

"Exactly my point! Rumor has it Leonard messed with the books so he could siphon off the money for himself."

A possibility, Ella knew, but one she didn't want to consider. The Leonard she knew had been irresponsible but he hadn't been a thief. Not that she knew of.

What if Nathan was lying to turn her suspicions elsewhere? The thing about his truck being returned the same night it had been stolen was pretty convenient. If it ever had been missing in the first place.

Ella would like to test him psychically to see if she could tell what was going on in his head. But even if it was possible—and she wasn't sure she could manage it—Ella was certain he would know. Nathan might not be a shaman, but he undoubtedly had some power left.

Considering he was in the mood to talk—to place blame—she decided to take advantage of the situation. She sat in the chair opposite her cousin and leaned forward to draw him in.

"Nathan, do you think Leonard has ever used what he learned from Father to his own advantage?"

"Leonard's no shaman."

"No, but that doesn't mean he wasn't messing around with his powers."

"To do what?"

"I don't know." Ella needed to be careful how she questioned Nathan. She didn't want him to know *he* was suspect. Not that she wanted him to be guilty of anything. "What about in the past? Did Leonard ever do anything he shouldn't have?"

"Who hasn't?" Nathan took a swig of his coffee, then set down the mug. "What are you getting at, Ella?"

"I've just been doing some thinking, Nathan. Those terrible things that happened on the rez fifteen years ago—you know Father wasn't responsible."

"So now you're thinking Leonard was?"

"I don't know who, but someone else was. You're the one

who brought up Leonard. I've been thinking Jimmy has a lot to answer for myself."

"Why Jimmy?"

"Because he was part of the crowd that murdered Father."

"I couldn't believe it, either, but Jimmy seemed convinced Joseph was responsible for the bad things that were happening. To tell the truth, Jimmy wasn't himself that day. None of them were. It was like they had some weird fever."

Ella remembered thinking the same thing. "Did Jimmy ever say anything against Father to you?"

"What is this, Ella? What are you doing? Why are you trying to place blame now?"

"You warned me about Leonard. Why did you do that?"

"Because I'm concerned."

"So am I."

From the look he gave her, Ella knew he was concerned about her. What she didn't know was whether that was a good thing or a bad thing.

She did know enough to back off. Of the three men who'd apprenticed with her father, Nathan was the most complex. He'd lived in his father's white world for years after going to college, yet he'd not only come back to the rez, he'd become an activist with a militant Native American organization.

Was her cousin wrangling horses for *Paha Sapa Gold* because he needed the money, or because he wanted to keep an eye on the goings-on of the movie company?

And why?

To make sure the Lakota were represented accurately or to have the opportunity to make bad things happen?

What would be the point?

Ella wondered if Nathan didn't like the focus of the movie that was being made partly on rez land.

If so, then what was he going to do about it?

Chapter Nine

After a restless night filled with haunting snatches of the past that even awake put him on edge, Tiernan got up before dawn and was glad to see that Ella had done so, as well. They shared a quick cup of coffee and some cold cereal, then headed for the reservation before parting ways.

Worried about Ella, Tiernan stewed at the gas station, waiting for it to open. But finally he got the new tires and hauled himself to work. He thought about the stubborn woman and their investigation all the way there.

Was he letting his past blind him, making him incautious and therefore putting her in danger?

If his wanting to make up now for what he hadn't been able to resolve then got Ella hurt, Tiernan would never forgive himself.

He was still worrying when he arrived on set and checked each and every one of the MKF horses. Thankfully, none of them were sick.

But he did have the unpleasant duty of telling his supervisor Doug Holloway about the problem.

"Good grief, we're doomed. We've just started and already we're lost." The first assistant director spoke in a stricken tone and, when Tiernan simply frowned in response, explained. "We're going to have a continuity problem."

"Continuity?"

Doug punched at his little round glasses. "We used those horses in the sequence we shot yesterday, right?"

"Three of them," Tiernan agreed.

"You have look-alikes? If not, you'd better find some or we're going to have to reshoot. That would not be good. Reshooting costs money. *Big* money. Max would be hacked off if that happened," he said of the director.

About to protest that they'd only used the horses one day, Tiernan saw the look on the other man's face and kept that thought to himself.

"All right, the chestnut and dun shouldn't be a problem, but the Paint's face had unique markings. I don't have another horse that looks anything like that."

"You just need the coloring on the face to be adjusted?"

"That would be the main thing."

"Go see Carrie Albright, the makeup artist, and see what she can do. Before this movie is over, I'm going to have an ulcer. Or lose more hair."

Makeup on a horse?

Again Tiernan said nothing, simply followed orders and went in search of the makeup tent.

All the while he looked for some sign of Ella. Passing the parking lot, he didn't see her SUV. She would be all right, he told himself, because she would be careful after what had happened the night before. And he needed to concentrate on work for the moment.

Color was sometimes used to highlight a show horse's features, he knew, but what they needed was a transformation. That, he'd never seen done.

Inside the makeup tent several tables were set up with

products. The tent was empty but for a small woman with wispy brown hair around a narrow face that appeared ageless. He assumed she was Carrie Albright and introduced himself. She smiled, but not much on that too-perfect face moved.

Staring in fascination, Tiernan said, "Doug Holloway sent me to see you."

Narrowing her gaze in return, Carrie said, "Huh, haven't noticed you around before. Did they just hire you? Are you playing an army man or a civilian?"

"I'm not one of the actors—"

"Too bad." She grabbed his chin with a ring-laden hand and turned his head from side to side. "Good bones. The camera would love you."

When she let go, he said, "I am needing your makeup skills…for a horse."

"A horse. Why?"

"A couple of our horses came down with the flu yesterday. One of the horses already filmed is a Paint with a uniquely marked face. I don't have another who could pass for him. Doug thought maybe you—"

"Could make one horse look like another? Okay, let's see what we have."

Tiernan led her to the pasture and pointed out Bandit, the horse most like the one that needed replacing. Carrie quickly sketched the horse's markings.

A few Lakota extras gathered round to watch.

"That a special horse?" the one named Bear Heart asked.

"Hopefully, he will pretend to be someone else."

"No different than any other male, eh?"

Tiernan grinned at the old man who always seemed to have a sense of humor. "No woman involved, though. Except for her," he said of Carrie.

She then took him to the camera crew and asked for the

video back up from the day before so she could see what the sick horse looked like.

Peering over her shoulder, Tiernan watched Carrie make a quick sketch of the Paint's face. She was careful to get the markings exactly right. Then she sketched the poll, neck, shoulder, chest and legs, as well. The detail in her sketches was meticulous.

"Do you think you can make it work, then?" he asked.

"You must be joking. This is child's play for any decent make-up artist. We transform actors into someone they're not. For example, I could make you up to look like…well, practically anyone here," Carrie said, indicating the crew members of different ages, weights and races milling about. "Give me a little time to get what I need—someone got into my tent and made a mess of my things, so it may take me a while."

"You mean, they went through them?"

"Everything was thrown around like someone had a temper tantrum. Anything like that happens again, I'm going to request a security guard!" She sucked in a big breath. "You bring the horse over to the makeup tent in an hour."

It would probably take half that long to get Bandit, halter him and lead him back here. Tiernan considered using restraints since horses often freaked at anything new being done to them, but he didn't want to hobble Bandit or use a twitch or ear restraint, not when he had other methods of handling him.

As he walked back to the pasture where he'd left the horse, Tiernan thought about the makeup tent. Who would have been in there messing around? Some kid?

After rounding up Bandit, Tiernan clipped a lead to the halter and then hand-led the spirited horse to the gate, all the while touching him and tuning in, making the connection that would convince the horse that he was safe, not an easy task when working with a prey animal. Getting a jump on the

Paint's fight-or-flight instinct before it took hold was key. Tiernan could only imagine the horse's response to what was about to happen to him.

By the time they arrived at the makeup tent, and Tiernan secured Bandit's lead to a nearby tree, he was confident that he and the beast had bonded.

Carrie came out of the tent, carrying a box. "Ah, there you are. I'm ready. How's our friend?"

"As settled as I could manage."

Referring to her sketches, Carrie first lightly chalked in the new color design wherever needed on the Paint's hide. All the while, Tiernan stood next to the horse, touching him with a steady hand, using their unspoken connection to keep the horse calm.

Then Carrie slipped on an oven mitt and dipped it into a pan of brown dye. Patient until then, Bandit rolled his eyes and Tiernan sensed the immediate desire to flee.

"Nah, nah," he murmured, stroking the horse both physically and mentally until Bandit settled.

"You have quite the control there," Carrie said, using the dye on the mitt to create the basic shapes of the pattern on the horse's hide.

"'Tis a gift," Tiernan said with a grin.

Even so, Bandit's flesh shuddered, and Tiernan concentrated, put thoughts of a pretty pasture on a lazy spring day into the horse's mind. Bandit stilled just as Carrie took a soft cloth with some petroleum jelly and blended the color to make it look more natural. But a moment later, when she went at his face with a toothbrush with a squeeze of white paint from a tube, the horse sidestepped.

"Easy now," Tiernan murmured, rubbing the horse's ear between two fingers just as the producer and director of the film walked by, hot in the middle of an argument.

"Sorry, Jane, it'll take too much time."

"You said we would do this my way, Max!"

"I've rethought it and decided against it."

Bandit settled and let Carrie work in the white paint.

"You *promised!*" Jane said.

"Too costly. I already took a bath having to get another camera after one of ours mysteriously melted down."

Something had happened to one of the cameras? And this after the makeup tent had been messed with. Tiernan wondered if the camera meltdown was something that just happened…or was planned….

"That'll be covered by insurance," Jane argued.

"Look, I don't have the insurance now, and I need the extra money for the mine scenes. Getting some of that equipment in when we shoot the gold scenes is going to be far more costly than what I was originally quoted. As will be the big cleanup after I blow the mine's entrance as part of the act-two plot point."

"Then we can change—"

"Jane, enough! I *am* the director."

The producer flushed with color and looked away.

Tiernan hadn't known they were going to blow up the mine entrance. He wondered how stable the mountain was in this area, and whether such a move would cause more problems than the director was even aware of.

The producer and director passed Tiernan.

Their emotions flared—desire, resentment, power. Realizing they were more than coworkers and had a serious relationship, he suddenly had a fleeting image of Ella in mind. Tiernan closed himself down and concentrated only on the horse as Carrie used hair spray to set the color.

The last thing he wanted to think of was dealing with a relationship with someone he could love. Not when he could never have that for himself.

WIND SWEPT AROUND the hills, whistling through the pines and pummeling the entrance to the abandoned mine…his favorite place to journey. This day, he would not travel alone. He wished his companion to see with unfettered vision, to experience with a truly open mind for the first time. He'd been cultivating her for this moment.

He shook the drug from his leather pouch into the palm of his hand and offered it to her.

Dutifully, she accepted the tablet and put it to her ripe lips. Her hair fluttered around her face as her gaze locked with his, and she tongued the drug as she would soon tongue him. Then she rolled the drug into that clever mouth and with a little moan that made his groin tighten, swallowed and smiled at him—not the pure smile of the innocent, but one artful and calculating. She licked her full lips, knelt before him and thrust forward firm breasts straining at her thin blouse.

He'd tasted those breasts before, had suckled her until he'd been blinded by desire. "Strip," he commanded, sitting and closing his eyes.

He could see her in his mind.

She gave him a calculating look, then sat and pulled off her boots and socks. Such beautiful feet, long with perfect toes and the nails painted a deep red that reminded him of blood. She slid a bare foot along his inner leg to his groin and raised her knee so that he could see she wore nothing beneath her skirts. The sight made him catch his breath.

She smiled and raised her hands to her shirt. Unbuttoning it took an agonizingly long time.

"Hurry," he urged, his mind already expanding for the journey.

The sun hung low in the sky and dispatched shadows that careened from crag to crag around them until the very rocks awakened. Was she aware yet? Did she see the way the sun cast dying purple and chartreuse beams across the sky, behind the expanding clouds?

Her eyes dilated and her breath grew ragged and for a moment, she seemed surprised. Then she purred and spread open the cotton shirt and fluttered closer to him to offer her perfect breasts. A gift he couldn't refuse.

He twirled his tongue around the turgid flesh and opened his trousers to release himself for her. Smoothing her skirts up over her waist, he slid over her….

"Wait," she whispered, tightening her thighs, denying him entrance.

His senses were amplified and her voice echoed in his head as if the rising wind whirled through the tunnels of the mine. Desire slid through him like a molten volcano waiting to erupt.

"You have something more exotic in mind?"

"A trade. You can have whatever you want of me if you give me what I want in return."

He barked a laugh. Did she really think she could bargain with him? It amused him to let her think she could.

"And what is it you want?"

"To have what you have. I know what you found."

"You're delusional…well, yes, of course you are." He'd made certain of that with the drug. "Now, spread your legs like a good girl."

Her thighs didn't open.

Her eyes were slitted, her nostrils flaring. "I want what you have," she said again. "If you're smart, you'll keep me happy."

Her words whirled through his mind with tornado velocity. "Threats?"

His instant fury made the earth rumble under them and the tunnel walls shake. Who did she think she was? Did she think she could control him by withholding sex?

"You need a lesson. I will teach you control." And then he

would be done with her. He captured her gaze with his and forced his will on her. "Now invite me in."

She had the good sense to look frightened and not try to thwart him again. Her legs fell open and he slid inside her. Her eyes opened wide with fright as he pushed himself to the hilt, then imagined himself continuing until he pierced her mind.

Exhilaration pushed him over the edge. The rush of his pleasure was like a river, washing through her and over her, making her imagine she was drowning. She gasped, her full lips opening and closing, her hands clawing at his back, as she fought for air.

He savored his work for a moment.

Then he opened his eyes and gazed at her directly. They were still in the same positions as when the journey in their minds had begun. She still knelt before him, her skirts modestly down, her blouse buttoned. But it was her eyes that gave her away. They were wild and unfocused. She was searching for something she no longer could remember.

Good. Then he was finished with her. He rose.

As he left the mine, a vision came to him. A woman far more interesting and complicated. He would enjoy playing with Ella Thunder before seeing her die.

Chapter Ten

Tiernan arrived at refuge headquarters after a grueling day on set—no fun having a recalcitrant horse made up several times since exercise made Bandit sweat and the white makeup smudge. There would be a few more days of shooting for Bandit, but at least the subterfuge worked and the stand-in easily passed for the sick Paint.

Tiernan parked the truck under a tree. Though he spotted Ella's SUV already parked outside the house, he headed straight for the barn to check on the sick horses. Once done there, he would throw himself in the shower and get ready for the engagement party.

He'd insisted Ella come, too. She'd protested at first, said she didn't belong, but then he'd claimed if she wouldn't go, neither would he, because she needed to be protected. That had convinced her. Though he would probably be too tired to fully enjoy the event, he would enjoy her company despite his reservations and would appreciate catching up with family, especially a couple of first cousins he'd never met before because they'd never even been to Ireland.

Kate was just about to leave the barn when she caught sight of him and waved him over. "Tiernan! You won't believe it, but the horses are fine now—like they never were sick in the first place." Her curly red hair was practically bristling as if she'd been spooked.

He rushed past her and went from stall to stall and confirmed for himself that the horses looked perfectly normal. A couple were even munching away at their food. Amazed at the change in the horses, he rejoined Kate who still stood in the doorway, wearing a mask of confusion.

"Perhaps we caught the problem just as it started," Tiernan said. "Or perhaps it wasn't as bad as it sounded." And the horses' coughs had sounded as serious as any he'd encountered before.

They started for the house together.

Kate said, "Okay, here's the really weird part. I got the results from the lab. Nothing. No virus. No bacterial infection. *Nothing.* When I took those samples, those horses were completely healthy according to the tests."

A strange feeling shot through him. "'Tis odd, indeed."

"More than odd."

They stopped and stared at each other. Sensing Kate was blocking herself from what could be a logical explanation, Tiernan was the first to break the thick silence.

"Perhaps the horses were never sick at all, simply made to appear sick."

"How? By magic?"

He didn't miss the irony in her tone. "I'm thinking sorcery."

"You mean…Lakota?"

He nodded. "Executed by whoever left the raven's track on the post." Someone very good at shielding, because he hadn't sensed anything abnormal the night before. Then, again, he hadn't been looking for anything other than a way to help the horses. "Perhaps he thought making some of the horses *seem* sick would panic everyone and stop the production for a couple of days, putting the film behind schedule."

"Time is money," Kate mused, starting off for the house again.

"But you and Chase got the horses out in time before anyone even noticed."

"And the magic wore off?"

"Something like that. Possibly the spell was specific to the horses staying in that pasture, the symptoms spreading from one to the other like a real virus, and when you removed the sick horses, you broke the spell."

"Not that it seemed broken last night."

Tiernan sighed. "Perhaps spells simply take time to wear off. I wouldn't know since I've never encountered one of this sort before, but I've seen some unusual things."

"Someone else in the family might be familiar with this kind of thing," Kate mused. "I mean, a bunch of McKennas will be at the ranch tonight."

"But you're not going to tell them anything."

"Why not?"

"And ruin your brother's engagement party?"

As they stepped into the empty reception area, Kate said, "Be reasonable! We might be able to stop whatever is going on, you know, if we combined all our psychic abilities—"

"'Twould be a disaster, for certain! Too many cooks…" Someone was bound to get hurt. "Leave it alone, Kate. Leave it to me."

This was something he could manage without having McKenna backup. For the first time Tiernan could remember, he would be his own man. No one to answer to. He would get to the bottom of the mystery. For Ella.

And for himself.

ELLA WAS GLAD not to be left alone, but still she felt strange attending a party for someone she didn't know.

"Are you sure this is okay?" she asked when they left the truck. Her feet stopped, didn't seem to want to move. "Your bringing me—did you ask your cousin if it was okay?"

"Rose and Charlie will be delighted to have your company. Why are you so nervous?"

Was it that obvious? "It's just that I don't like intruding, McKenna," she said lightly. "I don't know anyone here." And undoubtedly they'd be looked at as a couple, which made her doubly uncomfortable.

"You know *me,* Thunder. I am not acquainted with half the people here, either, so you are doing me a great favor by accompanying me." He slipped his fingers through hers and gave her a light tug. "Come on."

The touch shot a thrill through Ella. She followed Tiernan's lead, taking a brick walkway past the big front porch and around to the back of the two-story house, painted white with green trim. Flowering bushes with white and yellow roses made a beautiful natural fence along the walkway and continued all the way into the backyard.

Today, clean-shaven, hair slicked back from his roguish face, wearing tan trousers and a crisp white shirt open at the neck, Tiernan not only fit the groomed grounds but made Ella's pulse rush a little faster. She rarely spent time in the company of such an attractive man. Not that they were on a date—Tiernan had made it clear that their being together was strictly for her safety—but she couldn't help smiling.

Tiernan's relatives were gathered on the back patio. The smells that wafted from the big, brick barbeque made her stomach curl in anticipation. And the tables loaded with side dishes and desserts were equally enticing.

The Farrells and McKennas made a big noisy group, everyone talking and laughing at the same time. Tables were set up for the party—two big picnic tables with benches and a couple smaller round tables with chairs. Several kids ran together, their hair different shades of red. Ella spotted three small girls who had to be triplets, barely school age. The other little kids were toddlers.

"There you are, Tiernan, lad," said a woman with fading and grayed red hair. She turned her shining smile on Ella. "And you must be Ella. I'm Rose."

"Thank you for having me."

"Ah, no problem at all. I'm just glad my youngest son is finally going to settle down and in this area—a real cause for celebration," Rose said, a slight hint of Ireland in her speech. "So the more the merrier, as I always say."

Tiernan nodded. "Rose took me in never having met me before."

"Family is family, and there's always room for another McKenna." She pinched Tiernan's cheek and gave Ella a wink. "Good to meet you. Tiernan, make the girl feel at home, if you would."

"I shall do my best."

Rose went off to greet more arriving guests.

Ella said, "She's very nice."

"That she is. I could use something to drink."

Which meant Ella met more of Tiernan's cousins since Kate's brother, Neil, was playing bartender and his wife, Annabeth, was assisting. Neil was a buttoned up kind of guy, but Annabeth seemed earthy, especially when her toddler son, Jeremy, ran up and threw his little arms around her legs. Annabeth picked him up and smothered him with kisses. Then, to Ella's surprise, Neil put his arms around them and kissed them both.

"You need to get yourself a wife and kids," Neil told Tiernan. "Your life will change forever."

"'Tis what I'm afraid of," he said, and though his tone was light, Ella got the distinct feeling that he wasn't joking.

"Forget all that McKenna prophecy stuff," Neil said, then added, "Kate told me, asked me what I thought, and—"

"Another time." Tiernan said stiffly.

As they moved on to the food line and loaded plates with potato and bean salads and corn on the cob and fresh fruits, and a chunk of corn bread, Ella found herself covertly peering at Tiernan, trying to figure out what was going on with him.

What kind of prophecy had Neil been talking about?

Before she could analyze what she was feeling, she met cousins from Chicago, who Tiernan didn't know—Skelly and his wife, Roz, parents to the triplets. The sea of faces began blending together in her mind by the time they got to the brick grill where chicken and ribs and small steaks were cooking.

Just as she was about to reach for ribs that had been put off to the side but close enough to the coals to keep them warm, a flume of fire roared up from the grill and Ella dropped her plate.

"Hey, are you okay?" Tiernan asked.

Ella nodded. "The fire…it scared me, is all." Her pulse was still whacked out, the blood rushing through her so fast she could feel it throughout her body. Taking a deep breath, she calmed herself down. "I'm afraid I made a mess."

"Here, I'll take care of it. Take this," he said, handing her his plate, "and go sit down. It'll just take me a few minutes to load up another."

Normally she would have insisted on helping, but the area was crowded with family members who were all giving her curious looks. Crushing her left arm into her side, she hurried to a small empty table with a big red-and-green umbrella at the edge of the crowd.

She looked over to see Tiernan trash what she'd spilled. Then he wiped his hands, picked up another plate and started piling it with more food. He filled another with barbequed chicken and ribs, then joined her.

"Oh, Lord, can we really eat all that?" she said with a breathy laugh.

Her embarrassment eased when he grinned at her and said, "We can but try."

When he sat, she picked up a tempting rib—the meat practically fell off the bone. "You don't even know how lucky you are to have such a big family. I'm a little overwhelmed and a little jealous, too. Mother's parents are dead and she has one sister who never married." Taking a bite, she said, "I have the grandparents on the rez, of course."

"And your cousin, Nathan." he reminded her.

"And Nathan," she agreed. "Though, I honestly don't know how to feel about him."

Tiernan set a stripped rib bone on his plate and picked up another. "You do know Nathan was at the casino last night, do you not?"

"I didn't know until this morning. I never saw Nathan in the casino, but he saw me with Leonard and warned me off the man."

"He might have a point," Tiernan said. "*If* he is not the one stirring up trouble. I saw him at a poker table when we were walking to Leonard's office. By the time we came out, he was gone."

"Giving him enough time to slash the tires…" Ella sighed.

As they ate, Ella quickly recapped her early-morning conversation with her cousin and the fact that his truck had been mysteriously returned. Gradually, Tiernan relaxed and was more of himself.

"Nathan seemed sincere," she said, "worrying about me getting sucked in by Leonard. So do I believe him or not?"

"I can understand your difficulty—a truck being returned

several hours after it was supposedly stolen is a bit of a stretch. But possibly it's true."

"Did Leonard really have enough time to slash the refuge truck's tires and then steal Nathan's truck between the time he left us and we left the casino? I'm still thinking Jimmy is a more likely suspect. He could have seen us arrive—he had enough time to do both before coming inside."

"Or it could have been Nathan."

"I don't know what to believe or who to trust," Ella said truthfully. "And I don't know how we're going to figure out anything more. I tried talking to Nathan about the past and either he didn't know anything or he didn't want to go there. I got nothing from him."

"Perhaps 'tis time to call on your sixth sense."

"I don't know that it'll ever be time for that."

Thinking about forcing herself to go to the scary place in her mind knotted her stomach. Suddenly losing her appetite, Ella dropped her fork, cleaned her sticky fingers with a wet wipe and sat back in her chair.

Tiernan ate in silence for a few minutes, then, his plate nearly empty, sat back himself. "I guess whether or not you call on your powers all depends on how important it is for you to know the truth."

"I want nothing more."

"Then you have some thinking to do on the possibilities."

"There are no possibilities," Ella insisted. "Whatever powers I might have had, they're gone now."

Even as she said it, Ella knew that wasn't exactly the truth or she wouldn't have had those brief interludes with her father. Something had been going on there, but it hadn't been in her control.

"You know my opinion on that. 'Tis a matter of your pressing the issue."

"I've tried, okay. I've tried and nothing."

"Perhaps you were too stressed. Or of a mind that you could *not* do it and therefore fulfilled your own fear."

Not knowing what to say to that—maybe it was the truth, after all—Ella was grateful to see Kate hauling two people to the table. Both looked amazingly like Tiernan with the same twinkle in their thick-lashed green eyes and the same easy grin. The man's hair was a blue-black, though, and the woman's a rich mahogany.

"Tiernan," Kate said, "I want you to meet more cousins who came from out of state. This is Aislinn, who came from Santa Fe, and her brother, Declan, who came from New Orleans."

"Glad to meet two of Padraig's brood at last!" Tiernan hugged Aislinn, shook hands with Declan.

"What do the two of you do?"

"I run an art gallery," Aislinn said.

Tiernan looked to Declan.

"Just some of this and that," Declan said mysteriously.

Which interested Tiernan, though he didn't pursue it. Instead he turned to Ella. "Their da and mine are Irish twins."

Aislinn laughed. "But Da always says he's the better-looking one."

"So they're not identical?" Ella asked.

"They're not twins at all," Declan informed her, then explained, "Irish twins just means they were born in the same calendar year."

"Did you both come alone?" Tiernan asked.

"I tried to get Hugh to come with me, but our brother is a workaholic."

"I'm the only one in the family in New Orleans, so yes, I came alone, too," Declan said.

"You're not married, then?"

Aislinn and Declan shared a significant look then shook their heads.

"None of Padraig's brood has crossed that crevasse," Aislinn said.

Tiernan sighed. "I understand."

But Ella didn't. She only knew they seemed to share some secret knowledge. She felt more and more left out, especially when the cousins bonded, Tiernan seeming to want to know about New Orleans and Santa Fe, Aislinn and Declan wanting to know about Ireland.

Leaving Ella to think about Nathan's morning visit once more and to wonder again if her own cousin could have tried to run her off the road the night before.

And if so, why?

What could he possibly be up to?

Chapter Eleven

"I never thought I would see the day my little brother settled down," Neil McKenna Farrell told the crowd who gathered to toast the couple. "I wasn't even sure I would ever see him again, not knowing he was working undercover for the Feds on a case that had its own *personal* rewards."

Tiernan studied the new couple. Quin didn't look anything like the other McKennas present. He was big, tough, scarred, scary. Even so, Luz Delgado, the exotic beauty cradled in the crook of his arm, seemed to be his perfect match. Their love came at him in palpable waves, and the way Luz was looking at Quin made Tiernan feel empty inside.

Unable to help himself, he glanced at Ella, another exotic beauty and one who tugged at his insides every time he looked at or thought of her. Her long, dark hair was free of the ponytail she usually wore. It draped her shoulders bared by a festive, beaded white top that left a naked strip above the waist of her slacks, but covered both arms to her wrists. Curious that he'd never seen her bare-armed. Studying her face, he noticed she'd subtly highlighted her best features—her eyes and her full mouth.

Realizing the trouble he would get himself into if he didn't stop, Tiernan tore his gaze away from Ella.

"But all that's over and your life is about to change for the better, Quin," Neil was saying. "Everyone is happy that you're moving back to South Dakota where you belong. And we can't wait to welcome into the family the woman who tamed you. Luz, you must be quite a woman to have made Quin there stand still long enough to lasso him." Neil raised his flute of champagne. "A toast to the lucky couple."

They'd saved the champagne toast for last, to go with dessert. Tiernan raised his glass with everyone else. Too aware of Ella standing next to him, he held himself in check. He'd always known he would never be able to find happiness with a woman he loved. He'd been resigned to it for years. So why was it bothering him now?

Maybe it was being among so many relatives who had what he couldn't—spouses and kids and a permanent home—and seemed completely happy. He was jealous of their good fortune, 'twas simple as that. As everyone crowded in on the engaged couple to give their personal congratulations, they got between him and Ella, pushing them farther and farther from each other. Just as it should be, he thought. Ella was talking to Roz and seemed right at home.

Suddenly Tiernan felt as if he didn't belong here.

He backed off.

Seeking to escape, he followed the path that took him to the other side of the house and a track of land with old-growth trees. The path took him to the stand, but once beneath the canopy of firs, the brick walkway downgraded to wood chips. He followed that for a while to a little clearing through which a spring-fed stream cut.

He sat on a fallen, half-rotten log and watched the water trickle by and around the rocks in its path, just as his life seemed to be doing. He, too, was aimless, searching for something he couldn't find, avoiding what he couldn't have.

Suddenly the hair at the back of his neck stood to attention. As if he'd conjured her, Ella was there. He felt her, didn't have to turn around and look to ascertain that she'd followed him.

Tiernan stiffened…waiting…cursing the blood that suddenly rushed through him explosively.

Keeping silent, Ella moved as lightly as the wind and sat next to him on the log. He was filled with her presence, every inch of him. Her being there simply added to the torture that had grown over the past hour. Yet, he wouldn't have her leave.

Finally, Ella asked, "What is it that's bothering you, McKenna?"

"I just needed to breathe, Thunder."

"I think it's more than that," she said softly, no accusation in her voice. "You haven't been the same since Neil said something about the McKenna prophecy."

She fell silent again, yet Tiernan felt pressured. He'd never told anyone outside family about the prophecy. Certainly not about his seeing what had happened to his aunt. He'd never wanted to. He especially didn't want to tell Ella, lest she think him ridiculous.

As if he'd spoken aloud, Ella said, "Whatever is on your mind…you can tell me. Of all people, I would understand."

Would she? He'd never wanted to share the details of the family curse with anyone, not until now. But the way Ella was looking at him…the way he was feeling about her…

Before he lost his nerve, he said, "I can never have what they have."

"Who? Your cousins?"

He nodded. "Do not doubt that I wish Quin every happiness. The same for Neil and Kate and Skelly and any other McKenna who has found his or her soulmate. 'Tis not for all of us…not for me."

"What isn't? Being happy? Does this have something to

do with Neil telling you to forget the McKenna prophecy? And then when Aislinn said none of Padraig's brood had married, you said you understood...."

"Neil should have kept his opinion to himself."

Ella didn't say anything, just sat quietly as if waiting for him to explain. When he stubbornly refused to go on, she reached out to him, slid her hand over his. Her empathy traveled from his fingers to his arm to his heart...and all without her knowing of the impossibility of his dilemma.

Heaving a sigh, Tiernan knew something was happening between them that he couldn't allow. He had to warn her off before they got too close to stop it. He had to drive her from him before something terrible happened to her.

"The prophecy goes back nearly a century," he said, "and ever since, the descendants of Donal McKenna have been cursed. We can marry, just not the ones we love lest we be responsible for their deaths."

"How would you be responsible?"

He told her about Donal and Sheelin and how the witch had cursed Donal's descendants to lose their loved ones if they acted upon their feelings. He told her about some of the McKennas who had challenged the prophecy and lost.

In a soft voice, she said, "People do die—"

"You don't believe me, then?"

"I think prophecies are what you make of them."

Tiernan laughed. Bitter. Remembering. "I have personal knowledge, Ella, something I can't deny no matter how hard I try."

"Someone you loved died?" Her voice suddenly held a tight note that hadn't been there before.

He nodded. "My aunt Megan. The woman my uncle fell madly in love with and married the moment he could have her...and just as quickly lost her."

Ella took a big breath and seemed to relax. "What happened to her?"

Suddenly the nightmare appeared to him full-blown on the back of his eyelids. He couldn't look away. Even closing his eyes, he could see that horrible day as if it were happening now.

"Uncle Ross and Aunt Megan took me and my brothers to their home for the weekend. I was seven, then. Aunt Megan needed to go to the butcher shop and I wanted to go with her to get away from Cashel—my older brother. We were almost to the shop when Aunt Megan saw this auto and grew very nervous, said she recognized the driver."

"Someone who made her afraid?"

Again he nodded. "Because of the Troubles." He could hardly breathe as he explained. "Aunt Megan was originally from Belfast. Her da and brothers were part of the I.R.A.—part of the violence—and she thought this man was a unionist who'd lost one of his children in a bombing. Thought her brothers were responsible." Empathetic even as a child, he'd felt her fear wrap him in waves, seen the dark vehicle shoot down the street straight toward them. "I remember the auto heading for us. I tripped and would have been hit if my aunt had not acted quickly, lifting me and throwing me out of the way…."

His voice faded as he saw it all happen again. A nightmare in living color.

"Then she was hit?" Ella asked, her voice soft.

Filled with the remorse that would never let up, Tiernan nodded. "I was sprawled on the pavement when the auto ran her down and then just sped away. That fast she was dead." He could see her again, eyes open, lifeless, expression slack. "'Twas murder, nothing else."

"How horrible. Did they get the man?"

His vision clearing, Tiernan looked at her. "The *gardai* didn't believe me, put what I told them to the wild imaginings of a seven-year-old. I had no name to give them. No description other than the vehicle was black. I knew what I knew, but to them it was nothing. It all happened so fast. If she had not tried to save me—"

"It wasn't your fault."

"Tell that to a seven-year-old."

He wasn't seven anymore and yet he couldn't shake the feeling that he'd been to blame. Even at a young age, his psychic abilities had been primed. So why hadn't that worked in his favor? If he'd at least been able to describe the man or had been able to tell the *gardai* the license plate number, perhaps there would have been justice for the poor woman. No matter how hard he'd tried to get beyond the trauma, he'd seen nothing that made a difference.

"So that's why you're so willing to investigate Harold Walks Tall's death."

"'Tis why I think every victim is owed some justice," he admitted.

Ella squeezed his hand and he squeezed back, running his hand lightly up the inside of her arm. Beneath the thin cotton, the flesh felt odd. Tight. Uneven. And suddenly the cotton-covered flesh burned his fingers.

Flushing, she moved her arm away from him. "What about your uncle?" she asked. "Did he believe you?"

Returning his attention to the story, he murmured, "Nah-nah, he simply blamed himself, said it was the prophecy that killed his Megan and he should have known better than to take up with the woman he loved. He never got over it, all his life said it was his fault. He was right, Ella. There is no room for love in a McKenna's life, not for anyone descended from Donal McKenna, that is."

"Are you saying you've given up on life?" Ella's forehead was furrowed and she tightened her grip on his hand.

"What would you have me do?"

He met her gaze and shut out the soft emotions she exuded for him. How had this happened? He'd meant to drive her away, not pull her closer.

"Fight for what's important to you, McKenna. Do whatever you have to do to get what you want!"

"Is that what you're willing to do, then, Thunder?" he returned. "To find the man responsible for your da's death?" He challenged her with the one thing he knew would put her back up. It was time that he called in that chip. "You could find the villain if only you would call up the powers your da shared with you."

"No!" Obviously upset, Ella flew to her feet. "And it's not the same thing."

"It doesn't seem so very different to me. The intent, that is." Tiernan rose, as well, and faced down the woman who had the power to make him momentarily forget himself. "You've already lost your da but fear to use the powers you inherited to get justice, which is what you want. I fear to love a woman because I can't condemn her." No matter how much he wanted Ella. "The evil has already happened in your life—your da is dead—so what do *you* have to lose?"

Her expression stricken, she gasped. "Myself!"

Swallowing, he touched her cheek and for a fleeting moment felt a stronger, deeper, more intense connection than he'd ever had with anyone.

Fighting it, he said, "Fearing being burned as a sorceress is understandable—"

Ella pushed away his hand. "That's not what I mean. I don't want to die, of course, but there are different kinds of deaths. If I try to follow in Father's footsteps, I don't know who I will be, what using those powers will make me."

"A whole person?" he challenged.

"What, you think I'm not whole now?" Her voice rose. "You think I'm wasting my life?"

She turned from him, but he grasped her by the shoulders. "I think the real you is hiding, waiting for release. I would see that…"

Her hands were on his chest now, pushing, as if trying to put him from her. But the secret, unspoken things her hands told him were exactly opposite. In reading her, he felt an arousal of things he, too, was trying to push away. A wanting as frenetic as what he read from her.

Suddenly Ella was in his arms, and Tiernan wasn't certain if he pulled her there or if she threw herself against him. All he knew was the rightness of the close contact—of the certainty that this was meant to be. That he was meant to hold her. Kiss her.

And then he was.

Her lips were soft and dewy and flush with emotion. A cry deep in her throat signaled her need and, without thinking, he responded, deepening the kiss until he tasted her soul. Mouths linked, bodies pressed together, he imagined them joined as one, unfettered by anything but pure emotion and raw desire.

He spread his fingers wide and smoothed the bare flesh of her back. His hands wandered lower, cupped the fullness of her hips and then of her derriere.

As his desire grew in intensity, so did his doubts. He fought them, tried to make his mind go blank.

…sorrow in love…act on their feelings…put their loved ones in mortal danger…

So ingrained was Sheelin O'Keefe's prophecy in his soul, that, unbidden, it entered Tiernan's thoughts and then spread like a cancer until it crowded out all else and shattered the moment.

Breaking the kiss, he pushed Ella away from him. "I'm sorry. I never should have—"

"You're sorry you kissed me?" she choked out. Blinking as if trying to get her thoughts together, she then shook her head and backed off. "Well, don't worry about it, McKenna. It was only a kiss, after all. It didn't mean a thing."

With that, Ella turned and marched away.

And Tiernan, who had spent half a lifetime avoiding such a moment, felt as if he'd been brought to his knees.

WHEN TIERNAN HAD caught up to her after saying he never should have kissed her, he'd appeared apologetic, but no words of apology actually crossed his lips. They'd both kept up a polite facade with each other for the rest of the evening, but Ella had been relieved when they'd arrived back at refuge headquarters and she could close her door on him and hide what she was really thinking—that she had feelings for Tiernan and was certain he did for her.

Only this prophecy he'd spoken of was so very real to him, they would never work it out.

The bedroom was suddenly claustrophobic, but if she left it, she wouldn't be able to avoid him, not unless she actually left the house. Quickly, she put on a light sweater. After waiting to hear Tiernan enter the bathroom, she cracked open the bedroom door and slipped out and through the reception area, then into the still night.

She'd always loved to be alone with the Black Hills after dark, and as a kid had often sneaked out to take solitary walks, so this was like old times. The dark sky still sparkled with diamondlike stars. The balmy air exuded a familiar spiced scent—the resinous odors of the evergreens. The hills continued to spew sparkling rivulets of clear, icy water tumbling down from the sides of the mountain.

Not that she was going to go far enough to find the streams she used to wade in or drink from. Content with feeling the night air gently lave her, Ella walked only as far as the closest pasture, then quietly wound herself into the board fence for a ringside seat.

The moon shone over a small band of mustangs gathered nearby. They grew restless with her presence, one whickering softly, another answering in kind, but as she remained silent and became one with the night, they settled down and dozed.

Seeing them reminded her of the not-so-sick horses. Had someone really cast a spell over them? Or had something in their food made them sick for a short time? She doubted the lab had checked for anything beyond the obvious virus or bacteria. What if those horses had ingested some plant or drug that made them seem sick? Was such a result even possible?

Or was someone with dark powers really at work?

It was all too much for her to deal with alone, and at the moment that seemed to be the case. She needed guidance. In the past, she'd been able to find it by communicating with the elements, making them sing and sway and whirl in return.

The People incorporated nature into their belief systems, honoring it with multiple annual dances to ensure not only rain and plentiful food, but fertility in the clans. All things animate and inanimate—like the earth and rock of the surrounding mountains—had a place in the cosmos. Life must be harmonious, and the mind must be free of evil thoughts.

But apparently at least one member of the tribe was going against the beliefs he was raised to respect, and in doing so, had brought the tribe fear.

Searching the heavens, wishing if she tried hard enough, she would find her father in the stars, Ella thought she saw his face for a few seconds, but as quickly as she imagined it, he was gone.

Are you there, Father? I need your help.

In order to find that help, she would have to journey, that

was clear. Even though her father had begun her education at a very young age, the very thought of executing that knowledge now made her stomach knot. If she never tried, never gave it her best effort, she would never know if she could do it. Perhaps now was good. No one to see her fail.

Not that Ella was really prepared—she had nothing but herself, no tools of magic—yet she knew it was possible if more difficult to manage.

Closing her eyes, Ella freed herself and opened her mind. Though she tried expanding her reality, tried breaching the place where her father's spirit dwelled, she felt empty inside, just as she had for the last fifteen years. The few times they'd connected, it had been an unconscious thing. Or it simply had been her imagination.

A nearby howl sent the flesh along her spine crawling and Ella dashed open her eyes and looked around wildly. She seemed to be the only one affected—the mustangs hadn't moved. Had she really heard the sound or was her imagination at play?

Calming herself by focusing and taking slow, even breaths, she tried again.

With eyes closed once more, she sought to explore the elements—she could feel the pulse of the earth, could hear the whispers along the wind, could visualize the sky expanding around her. Imagining taking flight, she raced, her feet cushioned by clouds, and moved through star-strewn fields slowly at first, then faster and faster, all the while searching.

Father, find me...speak to me...tell me what to do....

The laugh that echoed back at her in answer wasn't at all familiar.

Wasn't Father.

Heart thudding, she stopped short.

Who is it? Who's there?

No voice answered, but she felt a presence…no, a force. She wanted to believe this could be her father, trying to get through to her, but she knew otherwise.

What then, was she to do?

A confused Ella didn't know.

The force grew stronger…darker…and she grew more aware and more afraid. Her pulse jagged in warning and she sensed that just beyond some invisible barrier, the man who'd set up her father awaited *her.*

Ella waited, too, to see if he would show himself. Her throat tightened, her mouth went dry, her eyes burned as she stared out at the abyss before her.

Though she saw nothing, she felt sharp edges poke at her, try to get inside her…try to invade her mind….

Ella mentally backed away from the presence. She tried to get away, but it followed. Surrounded her. Threatened to smother her.

"No!"

Eyes whipping open, Ella tried to orient herself. The moon had gone under a cloud and the night was as black as could be. The mustangs squealed and she heard their hooves dig into the earth as they wheeled away from her, trying to escape whatever was out there, stalking them all.

The low, spine-tingling roar of a mountain lion sent her scrambling from the pasture fence.

Ella ran, headed back toward the house, moved as fast as her legs would carry her. The earth trembled with every step, and the presence seemed to surround her.

Someone or something was following her…after her…

She pushed herself until her limbs flew and her muscles screamed from the strain. She didn't stop until she reached the front door, still open a crack, the people inside unaware, probably sleeping.

Thinking of screaming for Tiernan and Kate—surely they could do something with their McKenna abilities—Ella couldn't get enough breath to make a sound.

She practically fell into the reception area where she firmly closed the door against her unseen stalker. Just as quickly as he'd presented himself, he was gone.

Shaking now, Ella stumbled to the kitchen. Instead of taking refuge in her bedroom, she went directly to the porch door where soft snores told her that Tiernan was fast asleep.

There she sank to the floor, her back against the wall, and waited for the sun to rise.

TIERNAN WOKE WITH a start. Something was wrong—he could feel it. But when he sat up and looked around he was alone, nothing amiss.

The house was silent. He was the first up. As such, he put on a pot of coffee, then while it dripped, wandered into the reception area and found himself at the computer. He sat before it and used Google to search for *"Joseph Thunder."*

There were few references to Ella's father, nothing significant. An article in the *Custer County Examiner* reported how Joseph worked with the sick and the poor on Bitter Creek Reservation. It was accompanied by a photo of the man with tribal elders, including Bear Heart, whom he'd met on the set.

Hearing footfalls on the stairs, Tiernan printed the article, then quickly folded it and slipped it into his pocket. He would read it later, maybe get some information that would help with the investigation.

Perhaps his being able to prove who the killer was would ease his own past just a little.

Chapter Twelve

Ella threw herself into her work the next morning in hopes of putting Tiernan—and whoever was trying to get into her head—out of mind. With only three hours of sleep to her credit—half on the porch floor, the other half in Tiernan's bed—she was running on empty.

"What do you think?" Jane asked, her words staccato. She seemed unusually uptight this morning.

"Everything looks good." Though Ella was having a difficult time focusing on the details, she forced herself back into the moment. "Just make sure you instruct the dancers they're not to cross the eastern line of the circle."

"What are you talking about now!"

Startled by Jane's prickliness, Ella took a big breath and forced a smile. "According to Lakota beliefs, all energy enters the Sacred Circle through the east. Therefore, the east must not be breached by the dancers."

"No one watching this movie is going to know that…or which direction is east, for that matter!"

"But the Lakota dancers will. If you have them go against their beliefs, they will be insulted. Ceremonies are meant to be performed in a specific way." Not wanting to say some of the dancers might walk off the set if the Ghost Dance wasn't done according to that tradition, Ella said instead, "I can't predict what they will or won't do."

"Oh, good grief, is there no end of the problems I have to deal with today?"

What in the world was wrong with the producer? Ella wondered. Jane was usually so laid back, so accommodating. It was as if she'd become a stranger overnight.

Then she spotted Doug Holloway. The first assistant director stalked toward them, stopped before Jane and punched at his glasses.

"We got a problem and Max said to field it to you. Little Fawn hasn't reported to makeup and we're scheduled to start shooting within the hour. Calling her cell takes me directly to voice mail."

"What?" Jane cried. "Have someone go get her!"

"I can do that," Ella quickly offered, knowing they meant Marisala Saldana. And she could use a little downtime away from Jane Grant this morning. Everyone seemed to be off today, herself included. "I know where she lives."

"Fine. Call me as soon as you find her. Then get her here as soon as you can!"

"Sure," Ella said, already running for the parking lot, her calf-length skirt swirling around her legs.

Not that she could know whether Marisala was home—remembering the request for the love potion, Ella thought the young woman might be with her mystery lover.

Still, it was worth a shot, so she drove back to the rez, all the while keeping an eye out for trouble. But whoever had been after her the other night seemed to be lying low. Because he thought she and Tiernan had been frightened into giving up their investigation?

Perhaps they had.

That is, perhaps *Tiernan* had.

Odd since it seemed that this was a sacred mission to him, a way for him to make up for the past. How horrible that a seven-year-old had felt responsible for a death, even more so since he hadn't been able to get anyone to believe the poor woman had been murdered. She wondered what would happen if they were able to get justice for Harold and her father.

Would Tiernan feel as if he'd made up for what he couldn't do for his aunt?

Not that he'd mentioned anything about looking further into the deaths since the kiss….

Ella hadn't told him about what had happened to her the night before. She'd dozed a bit and then awakened before sunrise and sought her own bed. Even if she'd wanted to tell Tiernan, there hadn't been the opportunity. Over breakfast, he'd avoided talking about their investigation.

Ella couldn't stop thinking about it, though, couldn't stop wondering what exactly had triggered someone to kill them. Had she and Tiernan gotten too close? Questioned the wrong person? Leonard Hawkins?

She might be on her own now, but Ella wasn't ready to let go of the past until it was resolved. Staring at the road ahead, she felt her head go a bit light.

What do I need to do?

You know what to do. You are my daughter. It is time.

Her father's voice—he came to her unbidden yet again. Ella's heart thumped and her mouth went dry. She gripped the steering wheel as she crossed the narrow expanse between refuge and rez where she'd almost been forced off the road the other night.

I'm not like you, Father.

You are more like me than you will ever know. I am proud of you, Ella. Fear is good, but do not let it stop you from facing your destiny.

Starting, Ella realized she'd entered rez land. Fear tore

through her like a bullet because it seemed she couldn't help but face her destiny.

If she tried and failed…

Shoving the possibility—and the potential consequences—out of mind, she looked for a gravel road and turned onto it. Grandmother had told her Marisala lived alone in a trailer a half mile north. What she hadn't done was describe the trailer—a fancy double-wide with an awning, surrounded by a neat picket fence and a flower garden.

Marisala had claimed to have enough money to pay for the love potion. Apparently so. She lived alone and better than most on the rez. Once more, Ella wondered where the money came from. Ella hoped Marisala hadn't been doing anything illegal to afford the pretty place.

A convertible was parked outside the gate, so someone must be home. Ella pulled up next to it and hopped out. Thinking surely Marisala heard her, she wondered why the young woman didn't come to the door. A knock got no response. She tried again and wondered if Marisala had gone off with her lover in his vehicle.

About to go back to the movie set, Ella hesitated. Something didn't feel right.

"Marisala!" she called, slamming her hand against the door. "Open up, please!"

She banged again for a minute straight and was about to give up when she heard light footsteps. Then suddenly the door swung open. Marisala stood there, her expression slack, her gaze unfocused. Her hair was matted around her pale face, and her clothes were wrinkled as if she'd slept in them. She didn't seem fully aware.

"Did I wake you?"

Marisala blinked. "Ella?" she whispered, looking puzzled, as if she was confused.

"Who were you expecting?" Ella asked. "That man you told me about?"

Marisala shuddered but didn't answer.

Ella's unsettled feeling deepened. "Hey, what's wrong?"

"Wrong?" the young woman echoed, seeming confused, almost as if she were asleep now.

Ella took her hands. They were as cold as ice. "Are you all right?"

Finally, Marisala focused. "What day is this?"

"Saturday. You were expected to be on the set hours ago."

"Oh."

Like a pale ghost of herself, Marisala floated to the kitchen. She moved slowly, deliberately, as if she were on automatic pilot.

So what in the hell was she on? Ella wondered. Or was it simply a hangover?

Following, Ella said, "You realize you're late for work, right? You're holding up production. If you don't get cleaned up and on set fast, they may replace you."

No matter that Ella put urgency into her tone, Marisala looked as if nothing was getting through to her, as if she'd had some bizarre break with reality.

In the end, Ella realized it didn't matter what she said. The young woman didn't need to go to work, she needed help. She bullied Marisala into making herself barely presentable and getting into the SUV.

It was then she saw something she'd missed going inside—a raven's track cut into the earth just outside the gate.

Furious, Ella marched over to the sign and stepped on it, obliterating it, just as she would like to see happen to whomever had left the horrid sign there.

What in the world had that person done to Marisala? Ella

wondered, remembering the day Father had died, and the accusations that he'd taken Nelson Bird's mind.

Was there really a connection?

She'd always thought Nelson had mental problems, but perhaps that wasn't the case. Perhaps the real sorcerer had for some reason taken the man's mind.

And Marisala's?

A very scary thought.

One that haunted her as she drove.

First the horses…now Marisala…both echoing things that had happened fifteen years ago.

Wanting to believe in coincidence, Ella kept her racing imagination in check and quickly got Marisala to the health clinic located in the government building. When they entered, Jimmy Iron Horse was standing in the hallway, talking to another officer.

Jimmy took one look at Marisala and said, "What the hell did you do to her, Ella?"

"Me? Nothing. I found her like this and decided to bring her to the clinic to get her help."

Ami Badeau was just leaving the clinic with her mother Hannah, who was coughing up a storm. When she spotted Ella with Marisala, she turned to Jimmy and said, "Arrest that woman! She's making people ill! Mother saw her the other day, and she's been coughing ever since!"

"Stop blaming Ella," Hannah said. "I'm old. Old people get sick."

"A lot of people have been getting sick since Ella *Thunder* returned."

Ella didn't miss the emphasis.

Jimmy asked, "Are you accusing Ella of putting some kind of a curse on your mother?"

"Well, look to Marisala," Ami said, indicating the woman

who stood there, a silent shadow of herself. "Marisala saw Ella the other day to ask her for a potion."

"How do you know that?" Ella demanded. As far as she was aware, no one had been privy to their conversation.

"Just so you know, Marisala told me." Ami turned back to Jimmy. "She was her usual beautiful, outgoing self before she met with Ella. But not now, is she? Look at her! Something *bad* happened to the poor girl," Ami said knowingly. "You should arrest Ella, Jimmy."

"I need evidence—"

"Then get it!"

"Ami, stop such nonsense," Hannah said, between coughs. "You'll have everyone thinking Ella is—"

"A *sorceress?*" Ami finished for her. "Like father, like daughter."

Heat shot through Ella and she said, "Father was not a sorcerer! He was a shaman, devoted to his People, doing only good. He committed no crime, but *what happened to him* was a crime."

One that had gone unpunished.

Ami helped her mother to the door. "Well, you heed my words, Jimmy," she said, lingering a moment and then shifting her vicious gaze to Ella. "The responsible members of the rez take care of their own."

Jimmy didn't respond, simply stared at Ella with those gray eyes that spooked her. Was he holding back a smile of satisfaction? Or was that simply a grimace in response to the violence of the past?

Ami said people who'd been in contact with her had fallen ill. How many people? What kind of illness?

The responsible members of the rez take care of their own.

Had that been a threat? Was Ami suggesting The People might do to her what they did to her father?

Realizing that Marisala was making soft noises and swaying on her feet, Ella took hold of her and pushed her toward the clinic door without so much as giving him another glance.

She only wished she could dispel her growing sense of horror so easily.

BY THE TIME Ella returned to the set, the word was somehow out—Marisala had some bizarre break with reality. She ignored the questions from a couple of crew members and went in search of the producer.

Ella spotted Jane in conference with the director near the makeup tent. She hadn't gotten to the producer and director before crew and cast members gathered to bombard her with more questions, Tiernan included.

"What is going on?" he asked.

Before she could explain, an actor in full Native American dress demanded, "Did someone put some kind of evil spell on Marisala?"

A member of the crew added, "I heard someone is trying to drive the movie company away because this is sacred land." Directing this at Ella, he added, "And someone pointed a finger at you!"

Ella gasped and Tiernan placed an arm around her shoulders and came to her immediate defense. "Ella hasn't done anything, so cool down."

The voice of reason, Bear Heart spoke up. "Marisala has always been a wild girl. Perhaps she went too far this time."

Another Lakota said, "If you're wrong and the movie and all our jobs are at risk, then it's Ella Thunder's fault."

"Whatever happened to her, I had nothing to do with it," Ella said. "The clinic doctor is keeping her for observation."

She didn't add that he was testing her blood for unusual substances. Whatever Marisala had been into—or not into if some kind of magic was at work here—she deserved her privacy.

"We can't wait for her," Max said. "We'll have to recast." The director then suddenly gave Ella an intense once-over. "*You!* You can do it—you can be the new Little Fawn."

Horrified at the thought of getting in front of a camera, Ella protested, "I'm not an actress."

"There's not a lot of acting to the part. Besides, you have the looks for a romantic lead, and you're at least part Native American, so you'll do."

Tiernan tightened his grip on her shoulder, bolstering her decision.

"I'm sorry," Ella said, as pleasantly as she could, "but I won't be available."

"Then *make* yourself available."

Not liking the way the director was speaking to her, she held herself back from telling him so. "I'm simply here for a couple weeks as a consultant." Her pulse raced through her and she had a difficult time catching her breath. "That's all I'm willing to do."

A disgruntled Max seared her with a look, and Ella felt his anger like a tangible thing, but to her relief, he didn't continue to insist. What he did insist on was the crowd breaking up and getting back to work. Obviously not wanting to be the object of the director's anger, actors and crew members alike scattered.

"Gather the young Lakota women together," Max told Jane.

"We could shoot around Little Fawn," Jane suggested. "Marisala might be okay in the morning."

"We need a new Little Fawn. Now!" Max gave her his back and walked off.

Jane's spine went straight but she didn't say another thing as she followed him toward the set.

Ella found herself alone with Tiernan. "Shouldn't you be getting back to work, as well?"

"In a minute. When you are calm."

"I'm just fine."

"I can feel otherwise," Tiernan countered. "You are worried about the rumors."

A cold knot settled in the pit of Ella's stomach, but she argued, "It's not the first time I've faced them today, and it won't be the last."

She told him about the incident with Ami Badeau in front of the clinic, and about how Jimmy Iron Horse had spooked her once again. Then she told him about finding the raven's track outside Marisala's home.

"Perhaps you should stay away from the reservation," Tiernan suggested. "At least for now."

"How can I? We need to get to the bottom of this, Tiernan, before things get out of hand."

"The trouble seems to be spiraling already."

He was correct, of course. "All the more reason to get to the truth."

Tiernan didn't say anything at first. He stared at her, though, pinned her with his gaze. "Are you ready, then? Will you do what you must, even if it means using your powers?"

"I've told you before—"

"Aye, you have no powers. So you say. But I read you, Ella Thunder. I can taste your fear. I have offered this before, and I will do so again. Together, we can—"

"No! I can't! I tried and I couldn't do it."

Tiernan nodded and his concerned expression softened into something more neutral. "That is it, then, is it not? Ella, did you ever think about leaving? Going back to Sioux Falls?"

She started. "You mean *now?*"

"Perhaps 'twould be for the best."

Ella's breath caught in her throat. What was going on with him? He'd been distant with her since they'd shared that kiss at the ranch. And now he wanted her to leave? For a while she'd thought she didn't have to be alone in this, but obviously she'd been mistaken.

"I'm not ready to go anywhere," she said stiffly. "Not until I get some answers."

"What if you *never* get them? How will you feel then?"

She couldn't believe Tiernan was changing his tune, not when he'd been so positive about the need to investigate in the first place. Not when he had his own ghosts to dispel. She'd thought they were on the same page. Was he really concerned that she couldn't do anything unless she used her nonexistent powers? Perhaps he hadn't told her everything about his.

The very idea sent a chill through her—a chill dispelled by the memory of flames....

Still, she couldn't help asking, "What about justice for Harold Walks Tall?" And for her father.

"Perhaps 'tis not for *you* to do."

Nodding, she backed off. "You regret getting involved in something that doesn't concern you."

Perhaps he'd rethought his position on getting himself involved, at least not without her admitting to the powers he insisted she had.

"Ella, you misunderstand."

"Don't worry about it." These deaths didn't concern him personally, wouldn't drive away the guilt he held over Megan McKenna's unresolved murder. She turned away from him, saying, "I do understand."

"No, you do not. Wait!"

Ella was already heading for the parking lot, hoping to get away before her emotions got the best of her. She'd thought that she and Tiernan had a true connection, that they were on the same page.

Instead, he wanted her to leave it alone.

He wanted her to leave.

Now she had to face facts: if she wanted the truth, she was going to have to find it for herself.

Chapter Thirteen

Ella had totally misunderstood him, Tiernan thought as he watched her drive off. Her emotions had nearly spilled from her—hurt, betrayal, determination.

All he'd wanted was to see her safe. With her gone, he would find some way to learn the truth without putting her in danger. But apparently the only thing she was leaving was his presence.

Realizing that Bear Heart was still there and watching him, he nodded to the old man. "Would you have a moment to talk?"

"What do you need?"

"Do you know Ella Thunder?"

Bear Heart nodded. "Her grandfather, Samuel, and I are friends. I knew her father, as well. Sad thing, what happened to Joseph."

Tiernan indicated the canopied canteen area, now virtually empty. "Let us go get something to wet our whistles and talk a bit."

A few minutes later, they were seated at a table away from the food area that afforded them some privacy. Bear Heart stirred cream and sugar into his mug, and Tiernan sipped at his black coffee while he waited.

When the old man put down his spoon, Tiernan said, "I

fear for Ella's life. She will not leave the area, which would be the best thing for her considering what has happened since she arrived."

"She is stubborn like Joseph." The old man shook his head. "He wanted to face The People, to prove his innocence."

"You believed in him, then?"

Bear Heart nodded. "He was my shaman."

"Was he not everyone's shaman? What made the others think he was evil?"

"Fear. Superstition. Bad things happening on the rez. Things no one could explain. Then the rumors started. People whispering. Watching. Believing black magic tainted the land. Who else did they have to blame but the shaman?" Bear Heart took a sip of his coffee, then said, "Joseph Thunder did have apprentices." His dark eyes fathomless, he held Tiernan's gaze. "All three live on the rez now...."

"And bad things are happening again," Tiernan finished for him. "Do you think 'tis to drive Ella away? Or does someone want her gone for good?" He explained, "Whoever it is tried running us off the road the other night. Would Nathan Lantero or Leonard Hawkins or Jimmy Iron Horse have reason to want her dead?"

"You would know better than I."

"I have just met them. I do not know them."

"But you are the one with the power."

Tiernan started. He'd said the same to Ella. And like Ella had, he said, "I am no shaman—"

"Call yourself what you will." Bear Heart raised his mug in salute before taking a drink. "You might have power that whispers now, but it is simply waiting for the chance to shout."

Stunned into silence, Tiernan wondered if the old man could really feel or see some kind of weird vibrations around him. He did not think he wore his psychic nature like a second skin. While he was not ashamed of what he knew and what he could feel, and while he used his abilities as he could, he never thought of himself as having power.

"Do not deny it," Bear Heart said. "I am too old to be fooled."

"Fair enough. Then perhaps you will believe me when I tell you Harold Walks Tall was murdered."

Bear Heart appeared thoughtful, as if Tiernan's statement was no shock. "You know this to be true despite what your authorities say?"

Tiernan nodded. "We found the track of the raven where he fell. Ella and I did. The same sign that made your people think her da was evil."

"I have not heard this."

Even if the sheriff's men had noticed the sign, they probably wouldn't have thought it had any significance, Tiernan thought. Signs weren't part of their culture.

He said, "So the deaths seem to be connected…Joseph Thunder and Harold Walks Tall. But they were fifteen years apart. What did they have in common?"

Bear Heart shrugged. "Maybe nothing."

"I think there is, but 'tis something not apparent. Something they both had or wanted or knew," Tiernan said. "What can you tell me about Harold Walks Tall? What did he do for a living? Who did he do it with? Who were his friends? If we knew more about him, maybe we could surmise why he died, then track the reason back to Joseph Thunder."

Bear Heart thought for a moment, then said, "Harold did not work, not at any regular job that I know of. He had no family—they all left the rez. Or died young. As to friends, he did not seem to have any…though I did see him with Marisala Saldana more than once."

The unexpected connection hit Tiernan hard. "Harold and Marisala—"

"Were together." Bear Heart put his two forefingers together to illustrate. "At least it seemed so to me."

Tiernan's mind whirled. The raven's track had marked the place where Harold Walks Tall fell to his death…and Ella had found another outside Marisala Saldana's home.

"There must be a connection, then," Tiernan mused. "If you think of anything else that might be of interest, will you let me know?"

"I will be sure to send up smoke signals," the old Lakota said, then laughed to himself. From his pocket, he pulled a cell. "What is your number?"

HER COTTON SKIRT pulled up above her knees to cool herself down, Ella sat on a fence rail overlooking the refuge pasture closest to headquarters when Tiernan caught up to her.

"Filming is a wash for the day," he said. "We start again in the morning with a new Little Fawn." As if just realizing where she was headed, he asked, "You intend to ride?"

"That was my plan."

"Even if I have a new lead?"

Her pulse buzzed as she asked, "What?"

"Come with me and I will explain."

He waited until they were in his truck to tell her that he'd spoken to Bear Heart and had learned that there was some connection—probably personal—between Harold Walks Tall and Marisala Saldana.

"First Harold dies, then Marisala loses her mind," Tiernan said. "Obviously the murderer got to them both, though why the difference in what happened to them?"

"What if the villain doesn't like to dirty his own hands with murder?" Ella suggested. "Remember, he used the tribe to do his work there. Harold's fall might have been an accident during an argument. Or at least it could have been unexpected. But destroying Marisala's mind was a deliberate act."

"So that she would forget something the murderer didn't want her to remember?" Tiernan mused.

"Something she learned from Harold?" Ella thought about it for a moment. "You know, considering she and Harold were an item, she didn't seem too broken up over his death. Not only that, she wanted me to make a love potion for her, so Harold was barely cold and she was into another man. She said she was desperate to get power over him."

"The murderer?" Tiernan suggested.

"It seems so," she agreed. "And if that's true, then Marisala can tell us who he is."

"Do you think she will talk?"

"I doubt she can at the moment," Ella said with a sigh. If only she'd been able to get his name from the woman when Marisala had come to her. "I don't think she can remember anything of significance. You didn't see her this morning. She was like a shell, Tiernan. Empty. He did something to her mind."

"How do we reach her, then? There must be a way."

Ella fell silent. "There might be a way…if there was a shaman on the rez."

"You mean, use magic."

"Something like that."

They drove in silence for a bit, but Ella could feel Tiernan's unspoken questions.

Finally, he asked, "Do you know how to get the information from her?"

She shook her head. "I can't do it."

"Cannot or will not?"

"What does it matter?"

"I think you know the answer to that."

Ella clenched her jaw. If someone could bring Marisala

back, and if they could get the name of the man who took her mind, they would know who to fight. But she couldn't manage it even if she wanted to, Ella thought, remembering how she'd failed at doing something as simple as trying to talk to Father. So she just might as well forget it.

"There's no guarantee even if she regains her mind that Marisala will tell us who did this to her," Ella said. "Right now, I doubt she knows who she is. But maybe there's another way to find out. If we're lucky, her trailer will tell us."

Tiernan started the truck and they were on their way back to the rez in minutes. Ella tried to contain her nerves. No one would know what they were doing. Marisala's trailer was off the beaten path.

It looked exactly as she had left it. Even the smudged spot in the dirt where she'd eradicated the raven's track.

"Nice little place," Tiernan said. When they went inside, he added, "Looks like someone has been here before us."

A quick glance around and Ella said, "Nope, it was a mess before. I don't know if she always lives like this or if she simply couldn't deal with straightening up considering how flaked out she was."

"So where do we start?"

"How about I take the living area," she said, "and you take the bedrooms and bath."

Ella started near the couch where one short wall was lined with shelves, half of which were stocked with books. Now that surprised her. She hadn't taken Marisala for a reader. There were some mysteries and thrillers and many more romances—making Ella wonder if that's where the young woman got the love potion idea. One shelf held books on South Dakota and the Black Hills—everything from tourist books to topography—and on Native American culture and history.

Including the one she'd written for her students.

Is that why Marisala had come to her? Ella wondered.

There were no framed photographs sitting around, so she looked for a photo album but didn't find one. Not that the murderer would necessarily have wanted his photo taken.

"Find anything?" Tiernan called.

"Books. Nothing significant that I can tell. What about you?"

"Sexy lingerie. Perfumes. Oils. Marisala certainly indulged her senses."

Or the senses of a man, Ella thought, wondering what it would be like to indulge herself with Tiernan.

Flushing, she tried to put the thought out of mind. He'd apologized for kissing her, for heaven's sake. Even so, she had to remember that Tiernan McKenna was too much like her father. He might not be a shaman, but he relied on his sixth sense the way Father had—and he'd been pushing her to use the powers she had buried for all these years. Like her father, Tiernan would probably face down an angry crowd rather than take the safe way out. She didn't need that kind of risk taker in her life, Ella told herself, thinking of her mother. The poor woman had never been the same since her father had been taken. And the thought of something happening to Tiernan the way it had to her father filled her with foreboding.

Finding nothing of note in the living room, Ella started on the dining room. Not much here to look at—a small cabinet with dishes and a shelf collecting rocks of different shapes, sizes and colors. Ella picked up a small piece with a metallic luster that appeared to be gold. Iron pyrite or fool's gold was often mistaken for the real thing. That was Marisala's MO. Fooling herself into believing she had something that didn't exist.

Like a man Marisala thought she would be able to wrap around her little finger…one who'd destroyed her instead.

"Found something."

Tiernan reentered the room, waving something in his hand

at her. She set the fool's gold back in place and met him halfway. He opened his hand to reveal a beaded necklace with a gold buffalo.

Gasping, she asked, "Where did you find that?"

"On the floor next to the bed."

Even before she picked it up and took a closer look, she knew what he had found. "That's Nathan's totem." She swallowed her disappointment. "Nathan was wearing this when I saw him on the rez and on the set, so he was obviously here with Marisala since then." As difficult as it was to put it into words, she said, "Nathan must be the guilty one."

WITH THE DISCOVERY of the totem, their work was done, so they left Marisala's trailer and headed back for the refuge. As she climbed into the truck, Ella remained distressed and silent, her fingers picking at the fullness of her skirt. She didn't have to speak for Tiernan to know what she was feeling. Nathan was family, and as such, she didn't want to believe he was capable of turning a woman's mind. Or of murder, especially not of her da's murder.

"I thought I recognized the buffalo head," Tiernan said, starting the engine and moving off immediately. "Nathan was wearing it the day I met him. There was something about him…" He remembered being unable to read Nathan. He'd done his best, but Nathan had been able to stop him cold. "But I didn't think—"

"Neither did I. I questioned his motives and picked apart what he said and did, but I never really believed he could be so evil."

Tiernan noticed Ella rubbing the inside of her left arm as she spoke and wondered what had happened to it. She always wore long sleeves, and that one time he'd touched it, the skin beneath had felt unnatural.

"So what do we do about the totem?" he asked.

"I'm not sure. We don't have real proof that Nathan did anything, just that he was at Marisala's place in the last day or two."

Tiernan gripped the steering wheel hard. "Not any evidence that law enforcement could use to make an arrest." This time the eye witness was out of her mind.

"I can't see him working with Jimmy Iron Horse at all," Ella admitted. "Even if he's not the guilty one. Not that anyone in the County Sheriff's Office would believe someone could have the ability to take another person's mind. Marisala might have been self-centered and overly ambitious, but considering she grew up in poverty, who could blame her. She wasn't evil. She didn't deserve to be destroyed."

Tiernan reached out and covered Ella's hand with his. "Perhaps we can find a way to get it back for her. Undo what was done to her."

"I hope so."

Ella's emotions rushed through him and Tiernan knew she wouldn't rest until she found a way. She was angry and terrified and determined. And, he hoped, ready to accept her destiny—the powers handed down to her by her shaman father—because until she did so, Ella would never be truly whole.

"Until we can figure out what to do with the totem," he said, "I will ask Kate if she has someplace safe we can lock it up."

"Fine with me. In the meantime, I'm going to go back to the set, see what's going on," Ella said. "Hopefully they've found a replacement for Marisala."

Even if he was not psychic, Tiernan would be able to read Ella's true intent. Whether a new Little Fawn had been picked was of little interest to her and wouldn't cause the rapid beat in her throat.

"You will be looking for Nathan."

"I didn't say that."

Her tone confirmed his suspicion. "I will go with you, then, as soon as the totem is locked up."

"No," Ella said softly, her voice stiff, "I need to do this myself."

Though he wanted to argue that it might not be safe, Tiernan held his tongue. Arguing would only upset Ella further, so he would give her a head start, then he would follow to make certain she was all right. He wouldn't—couldn't—let anything happen to her. Even if he couldn't have her, his instinct was to protect her with everything he had.

When they arrived at headquarters, Tiernan walked Ella to her SUV.

"Let me come with you."

"No, Tiernan. I can take care of myself."

He slid his arms around her, murmuring, "I wish it to be so." Even as he wished for other things.

Ella clung to him for a moment and he thought to kiss her, but she suddenly freed herself with a flurry of discomfort. She couldn't look at him as she said, "I need to go."

And he needed to follow as quickly as possible, no matter what she said. He waved her off, then hurried inside to find Kate, who was making supper under the watchful eyes of Maggie, ensconced in the playpen where she was cooing to herself.

"Kate, I have a favor to ask."

"What is it?"

"Is there someplace safe to keep this?"

When he held out the totem, her eyes went wide. "That belongs to—"

"Nathan Lantero," he finished for her, telling Kate how he and Ella had found the necklace and the conclusions they had come to.

"I can't believe Nathan would hurt anyone. As for murder…" Kate shook her head. "I don't believe it. This must be a mistake."

"I hope it is, for Ella's sake. She went to find him. She would not let me come with her, but she cannot stop me from following."

Kate sighed and gave him a look filled with pity. "You're in love with her."

"I care for her welfare." Stubbornly Tiernan wouldn't admit to more.

"Love is what makes us who we are, Tiernan."

"Love is too dangerous for a McKenna."

"I'm a McKenna," she reminded him. "My brothers and cousins and I have our own legacy of love and danger left to us by our grandmother Moira. None of us found that love easily, Tiernan. We all had to face down danger and come out on the other side before we found our happiness."

Tiernan shook his head. "'Tis still different."

"Semantics," Kate said. "There's nothing in that prophecy that says you'll condemn the woman to die."

"Putting her in mortal danger is enough."

"But you can face the danger with her, Tiernan. If a thing is worth having, it's worth fighting for. You have to decide if Ella is that woman. Is she worth fighting for?"

"I've never met a woman I wanted more."

"Then tell her. Protect her if you must, but don't let her go, not if she's the one."

Tiernan thought about what Kate said as he left Nathan's totem with her and headed for his truck.

He would protect Ella with his life—no question about that—but he didn't know if he had the courage to tell her that he loved her.

Chapter Fourteen

Ella could hardly breathe when she arrived at the set and went in search of Nathan.

What would she say to him?

Having rehearsed her approach several different ways in her mind, she still hadn't figured a way to deal with her cousin that seemed quite right. If she accused him of crimes that he didn't commit, he might never forgive her.

And if he denied it, how would she know whether or not he was lying?

Would the abilities she had inherited from her father allow her to recognize truth, or could someone with developed powers obfuscate it?

The more she thought about it, the more Ella was convinced the key lay with Marisala. She could start by asking Nathan about his relationship with the young woman and see where that took her. She would do the best she could—whatever the result, whatever the danger she put herself in, she couldn't leave it alone. She *had* to know.

And if she learned the horrible truth, then what?

Who would she tell?

Who would believe her?

The sheriff's office would need hard evidence or a confession to pursue Harold Walks Tall's murderer. As to what had happened to her father or to Marisala—Ella was certain there was nothing she could actually do about those things, not unless Jimmy Iron Horse was willing to make a case to the tribal council. Fat chance, there, she thought.

Leaving the SUV in the parking lot, Ella went in search of Nathan. The area was more sparsely populated than usual, but plenty of people still milled about. Crew members busily checked over equipment and actors huddled in small groups, talking or running lines. She couldn't find Nathan, not with the horses or in the tack shed.

Spotting Bear Heart seated in the shade under a nearby tree, looking as if he was happily communing with nature, Ella walked over to him.

"Bear Heart, have you by any chance seen Nathan this afternoon?"

"Nope. He was around for a while but took off, said there was something important he had to see to."

Important? "Like what?"

"Didn't say."

"When did he leave?" Ella asked.

"Haven't seen Nathan since early this morning after he took care of the horses."

Which meant what? Ella wondered. That he'd been with Marisala that very morning before Ella had gotten to her? She swallowed hard.

"Thanks."

A sick feeling in her stomach again, Ella made for her SUV and the rez. If she didn't find Nathan there, then what?

She'd only made it halfway back to the parking lot when she heard shouts, and a handful of people rushed by her, a few running.

"What's happening?" she called, whirling to see where

they were going—and was shocked to see a cloud of black smoke a short distance from where she stood.

"Fire!" someone yelled.

Ella changed directions to go with the crowd straight to the town set and found that the saloon was on fire.

Seeing Jane Grant off to one side of the burning building, Ella raced to the producer's side. "What happened?"

"It's that crazy woman—someone said she went inside and started the fire."

"What are you talking about?"

"Little Fawn. Marisala."

Ella looked around but didn't see her. Several crew members were gathered around the building, discarded fire extinguishers at their feet.

"Where is she?"

"Inside," Jane said. "And she won't come out. The crew tried to put out the fire out but it spread too fast. We're waiting for the fire department to get here."

"That'll take twenty minutes, maybe more." Wondering how the disturbed woman had been let out of the clinic so quickly—not to mention how she'd gotten herself here—Ella rushed toward the building, screaming, "Marisala!"

The young woman suddenly appeared in an open window. She was crying and looking around wildly.

"Climb out the window!" one of several crew members standing in the crowd below yelled. "We'll catch you!"

Marisala shook her head. "No…no…no…" She didn't make a move. She stood frozen in the window opening, smoke billowing out around her, flames shooting up behind her.

"Marisala, listen to him!" Ella urged. "Come on, climb out of the window and jump. You'll be okay."

If Marisala were herself, she would have done it, Ella was

certain. But she stood there looking more confused and scared by the minute. Little mewling noises now escaped her.

Being this close to a fire made Ella want to mewl in fright herself. She closed her eyes and saw Father burning again and wanted to run away as far and as fast as she could.

"Someone went for a truck with a crane that should reach her," Max Borland said. Pacing, he looked all wound up. "But I'm afraid by the time it gets here, it'll be too late to save her."

Not wanting to see another person she knew burn to death, Ella moved away from the men and closed her eyes against the sight.

You can save her.

No, I can't, Father.

You have it in you to call on the power. It is time.

Swallowing hard, Ella knew it was now or never. She'd purposely avoided this...certainly didn't want to do it in front of witnesses. She hadn't forgotten how her father had been repaid. But if she did nothing, she would never forgive herself. She ignored her accelerating heartbeat and the inability to breathe and chose to try.

Focused on becoming one with the elements—Earth, Air, Water, Fire—the way her father had once taught her, she at first felt nothing. It had been too long. She was too afraid. The power simply wasn't there for her anymore.

Free yourself of what you know, Ella. Let your mind seek a higher plane.

Ella trembled with the effort. Her body ached as she tried to force her mind from the tangible world.

Relax. Do not try so hard. Drift. Feel the elements inside you.

Concentrating on her father's instructions, Ella tried with everything she had. The ground trembled beneath her feet, and the sky seemed to stretch, pulling in a bank of clouds overhead.

People around her gasped, and she heard a woman yell, "It's going to rain!"

Ella reached her mind up into the heavens. The wind picked up and the sky darkened and clouds piled up one on top of the other.

"*Aaiee!*" a Lakota woman near her screamed. "What is Ella Thunder doing?"

Ella gradually felt her mind shift.

Focused now, she tried to seed the clouds so that rain would fall, but all she got for her effort was heat lightning that lit up the sky all around them like an electric network.

The human agitation around her multiplied, but while she could feel the discontent and hear the sounds of voices, Ella could no longer see the faces or understand the words. Then thunder drowned out the babbling, but try as she might, she couldn't will the clouds to open and release the rain.

She lifted her face and silently prayed for a way to save Marisala.

Don't let another person die. Let me help her.

Wind whipped around her like a cloak and pushed her toward the burning building.

"Hey, stop! You can't go in there!"

A man rushed her as if to stop her himself, but when he reached for her, his hand went through her. Others made to join him to stop her, but Ella already crossed the threshold.

Heat blasted her, making her heart thunder, smoke tried to choke her and dried her mouth and throat, but she couldn't consider what she was doing, couldn't give in to her fear. She focused on Marisala to keep herself going. If she stopped now, the young woman would no doubt die a horrible death.

Flames licked at the steps. Her heart in her throat, she raced to them, took them two at a time, reached the second floor just as a terrified scream broke through the electric haze sparking her mind.

"Marisala!" she yelled. "Where are you?"

"Here!"

The sob came from the other side of a curtain of flame. Ella could barely see the trapped woman. Taking a deep breath, she closed her eyes for a brief moment. And then she stepped forward. The flames themselves were under her power, for even as she thought it, she was able to step through without the fire touching her.

Marisala was on the ground now, huddled below the open window. Her back was to the wall and she hugged her knees so tight she couldn't move.

"You have to get up," Ella urged.

Marisala mewled pitifully and curled up tighter.

Ella reached down, grabbed the other woman by the wrist and pulled her to her feet. "C'mon, you can do this. Climb over," she said, pushing Marisala onto the windowsill. "She's coming out!" she yelled at the men below.

As Marisala obeyed her, they formed a semicircle and one said, "We'll get you!"

But Marisala wouldn't jump, so Ella squeezed herself onto the windowsill next to the woman.

"Hold on to my hand." When Marisla grabbed on to her, Ella said, "Together. We'll jump together. On three. Okay? One…two…three…."

She jumped, and still holding Marisala's hand, pulled the woman along. Her head and stomach tumbled as strong hands caught Marisala….

"Ella!"

Tiernan's voice jerked Ella out of the trance. She opened her eyes to see Marisala being set on the ground. Relief filled her. It had worked! Her journeying had saved the girl—Ella had never actually moved from outside the building.

"Tiernan."

"Are you all right, then?" His arms snaked around her even as she heard the crowd rumble.

Whispers of her using black magic surrounded her and someone yelled, "Sorceress, free Marisala!"

"What happened?" Tiernan asked.

"Marisala jumped from the building." She stepped back out of his arms to take Marisala's hand. "I'm going to take her back to the rez," she said, hearing fire trucks in the distance.

"You can't take her anywhere," Max said. "A deputy is on his way to arrest her."

"Did anyone see the lass set the fire?" Tiernan asked.

"No," the director admitted, "but she was inside the saloon when it started to burn."

"Then perhaps in this situation she is the victim." Tiernan sounded reasonable and very convincing when he said, "Marisala will not be going anywhere in the state she is in. Let Ella take care of her and see to the rest later."

Max looked from Tiernan to Marisala and Ella. "All right, but you'll all be hearing from the sheriff himself," he warned them.

"So be it." Tiernan started herding them toward the parking lot as two fire trucks came into view. "I'll drive."

Even as Ella said, "No, I need to do this," something hard hit her in the shoulder. Her anger flared and, still hanging on to Marisala, she turned and stared through the crowd, somehow picking out the coward who'd cast the stone.

"*Aaiee!*" the man cried as he ran away from her.

"You need protection," Tiernan said.

Captivated by the emotion in his expression, she felt a physical response. Part of her wanted to let him put his arms around her and take her away from this insanity. But she couldn't do that and with things spinning out of control, she didn't want to see anything happen to him because of her. She hadn't counted on this.

So, regretfully, she said, "I have what I need. Go home, McKenna."

"I do not think so, Thunder. I am going to do whatever it takes to make sure you are safe. I have decided you're worth fighting for."

Warmth spread through her. "Let me take care of Marisala…then we'll talk about it," Ella hedged. She didn't know what she was going to do once she got to the rez, but she wasn't going to tell him that. "Please, Tiernan."

Reluctantly, he backed off. She could feel his energy buzz around her as she pulled Marisala through the crowd to the parking lot. She piled the young woman into the passenger seat and then, voices still buzzing around her, got behind the wheel and started the engine.

The last she saw of Tiernan was him with a small woman with wispy brown hair—he was waving a piece of paper in front of her narrow face, and they were headed away from the parking lot. Fast. What in the world was he up to? she wondered.

A banging on the car's hood and trunk put Tiernan out of mind for the moment. Lakota surrounded the SUV with threatening expressions and stances. Her anger flaring, Ella laid on the horn and slowly backed out of the space, gratified when two men had to scramble out of the way. She inched out of the parking lot. Next to her, Marisala moaned and rocked in her seat.

"Are you all right? You're not hurt, are you?" Ella asked.

"No." Marisala suddenly looked around as if she didn't know where they were.

"I'm taking you back to the rez, to Grandmother. Why did you leave the clinic?"

"Clinic?"

"Where I left you. Remember? I took you there this morning, because you weren't feeling well. They were going to take care of you."

Marisala shrugged her shoulders. "Nathan will take care of me. He promised."

"Nathan." The breath caught in Ella's throat. She could hardly believe Marisala had brought up his name herself. "So Nathan is your friend?"

She glanced at the other woman to see her nod.

"Is he your new boyfriend? The one you wanted the love potion for?"

"Love potion," Marisala murmured, her forehead creasing as if she were trying to remember. "Need a love potion…" Then she simply appeared confused.

Ella tried to get some clarity but Marisala wasn't up to making any sense. She hoped Grandmother would be able to help the poor woman. She could at least take care of Marisala while Ella found Nathan and did what she had to. There had to be some way she could make him take the spell off the young woman, could make him restore her mind.

As she drove through the rez, people left their trailers and houses to watch her. The hair on the back of her neck stood straight when she got to the center of town and people spilled from the casino and government building.

She pulled in front of the house and helped Marisala out of the SUV. "C'mon, let me help you inside. Grandmother will give you something to eat, and then you can rest."

Marisala was docile, didn't say anything, simply let Ella lead her to the house.

The door opened before they got to it. With a fierce expression on her leathery face, Grandmother held out her arms and pulled Marisala inside. Ella glanced back once and realized people had come out on their porches and others had stopped their vehicles to watch. An old familiar feeling sent a shudder of revulsion through her, and she slammed the door shut on prying eyes.

Grandmother got Marisala to sit in the living room and fussed over her to make her comfortable.

"Where is her mother?" Ella asked. "I'll go find her and let her know Marisala is here."

"Her mother died years ago. Starved to death," Grandmother said.

"Oh, my God," Ella whispered, some things about Marisala becoming very clear to her. No wonder she had wanted power over a man. She hadn't wanted to be abandoned again.

"What happened to this poor girl?" Grandfather asked.

"Something warped her mind."

"Something…or someone?"

"I don't know for sure."

Ella prayed she wouldn't have to tell them that Nathan—their other grandchild—was evil. She wouldn't do it yet, not until she was certain. A little spark of hope still burned in her breast that her cousin was innocent.

"Ella, I have some soup on the stove."

"I'm not hungry, Grandmother, but perhaps Marisala could eat."

"It'll be there when you're ready."

Though Ella didn't know that *she* would be here.

Going to the window, she peered out at the street, now crowded with people, all surrounding this house. Her chest went tight and she felt sick inside.

"What is wrong, Ella?" Grandfather asked.

"They think I did this." She indicated Marisala, folded in on herself.

"They think you harmed someone? Why?"

"Because they think I'm…like Father."

Indeed, it wasn't long before she heard someone shout, "Come out and meet your accusers, sorceress!"

The deep voice rumbled through the walls to get to her.

Though she was no longer thirteen, Ella felt a lump in her throat as she returned to the window and saw the familiar angry faces. She was hurt and afraid, but she was angry, too. Was this how her father had felt when he'd been betrayed by the very people he'd helped?

This couldn't be happening again.

"Come out, sorceress!" demanded a woman."Before we burn down your house!"

Ami Badeau! A lump in Ella's throat threatened to choke her, and her eyes burned as she went to the door. She couldn't let an out of control crowd hurt anyone else when it was her they wanted. That's why her father had gone out to reason with The People—to protect his family. Knowing she had to do likewise, Ella turned back to see the grandparents staring at her, eyes wide with horror. No doubt they saw the past repeating itself.

"Stop them, Ella," Grandmother said, her dark eyes shiny with wetness. "Do not let them do to you what they did to your father. Use your power to stop them!"

"I can't, Grandmother. You know that. The People are not evil. They are superstitious. Afraid. Possibly under the spell of the true sorcerer."

Like her father before her, she knew it wasn't right to use her powers for self gain, especially not if it meant hurting innocent people in the process. That was left to someone with evil in his heart. It had taken all these years to understand that. The People were innocent, victims of their own narrow lives and real fears, their minds twisted by the frightening things that had been happening all around them again. And, yes, they could be under the spell of the evil one, as well.

"Don't open the door!" Grandfather said.

"I must. It is my destiny to do this." Remembering Father's words, she echoed him. "It is time."

She felt it in her blood, in her heart, in her whole being. It was time to face her fears and somehow beat them.

The grandparents huddled together as Ella finally opened the door, and exchanged the safety of the house for the fear-charged dusk. Raising her voice, she said, "I have done nothing to any of you. I've done no evil—"

"Liar!" came several voices.

"We saw what you did on the set!"

"The fire started before I got there."

"Not the fire, what you did to make Marisala leave the building."

"What is it you think you saw?" Ella asked, looking around to those who'd been on the set.

A wide-eyed woman looked around wildly and told the others, "She made Marisala fly with her!"

Ella started. Through journeying, she'd made a mental connection with Marisala—had others been able to see what had been in their minds?

"Black magic! Evil!"

"I saved a woman's life!" Ella countered. "Someone else is at work here—someone who lives on the rez."

"Get her!" came an hysterical voice. "Keep her from hurting anyone else!"

No matter that she'd tried to talk them down with truth and logic, they weren't listening.

Two men grabbed her and Ella prayed that she could survive without resorting to magic. She couldn't hurt them—that wasn't the way, she reminded herself even as the frenzied crowd surrounded her and the men dragged her toward the church. Though she screamed inside, no sound passed her lips.

Wearing a venomous expression, Ami Badeau walked alongside her, saying, "I told you we take care of our own!"

This wasn't happening, Ella thought, her chest squeezing tight. Not again. Not to her.

She'd been so careful not to raise suspicions. Knowing using her powers would be dangerous, she'd refused until today, but she hadn't been able to let Marisala die.

Why couldn't they see that?

As had happened fifteen years ago, The People weren't themselves. Their faces had changed, their eyes burned with madness.

All but Leonard, who came running from the direction of the casino. "What are you doing? Have you all gone crazy?"

"We're taking care of the plague that threatens the rez," someone said.

Leonard argued, "Wasn't it enough that you killed Ella's father?"

"We destroyed but one evil," Ami reminded him. "She is following in Joseph Thunder's footsteps!"

Leonard tried to get between Ella and her captors, but two men waylaid him and dragged him away.

"You won't stop us," Ami said.

A man added, "It's the only way to cleanse the rez!"

As she was dragged along, Ella looked around frantically. Where were the tribal police to stop this madness? She spotted Jimmy Iron Horse in front of the government building. He wasn't with the crowd this time, but he wasn't trying to stop it, either. He stood, staring out at the scene, grasping the railing, his posture stiff, his expression intent.

Was he the one responsible for the green-tinged sky? Ella wondered, suddenly noticing the shift in the elements. The wind soughed and the earth itself tilted under her feet and the air grew thick with evil promise.

Nathan was nowhere to be seen! Was he sitting back and laughing over her plight?

Her gaze went back to the government building. Or was Jimmy Iron Horse manipulating them all?

Voices rose into a chant and Ella smelled smoke. One woman was dancing, another singing a death chant. She was pulled into the open circle and stopped before a post on which the track of a raven had been burned. Wood was stacked nearby, some of it already burning.

What should I do? Tell me!

Her heart thumped with a strange beat. As men with burning torches approached, her head went light. The flicker of power blossomed inside her even as she fought the two men who were holding her from tying her down.

Terrified, Ella felt her mind opening….

The sky darkened...the clouds stretched...the earth rumbled....

Then the pounding of hoofbeats made the crowd turn and split in two as a big red roan thundered through the town, straight for the church.

"Aaiee!"

"No, it's not possible!"

"He's come back for revenge!"

The rugged man seated on the horse had long hair decorated with a single feather and features as craggy as the Badlands. He raised bronzed arms as if he were going to strike them all down with magic.

People scattered, and one tripped, then screamed while trying to get away.

Ella couldn't believe her eyes. This couldn't be happening. Could it? What she was seeing couldn't be real.

Still, she whispered, "Father?"

Chapter Fifteen

"Take my hand."

Ella did as he bade. As they touched, her expression changed and her eyes widened. "You're not—"

Before she could finish and give him away, Tiernan pulled her up and she hooked one foot in the stirrup and swung her other leg behind him. Her arms wrapped around his waist and she lay her head against his back and his body responded with repressed emotion. Letting go of a war cry he'd heard from many a cinema sound track, he urged the roan forward and headed straight out of town. People had to jump out of the way so he didn't hit them. He didn't look back, didn't stop until they were far up into the hills and away from the insanity.

Only when he was certain they were safe, when he could no longer sense the evil that had overtaken Ella's old neighbors, did he look for a place to stop Red Crow. He found it in a dense area of ponderosa pines through which flowed one of the area's many mountain streams. A two-foot ribbon of water rushed over chunks of rocks.

Tiernan helped Ella dismount, her skirt fluttering up. 'Twas the gloaming, the time between day and night, and the forest made it seem even darker. Though what he wanted was to scoop her into his arms, he brushed her hair back from her face instead, looking for cuts or bruises. He couldn't see well enough to be satisfied.

"Are you all right?" he asked, hard-pressed not to check over every inch of her. That would require more touching than he could stand. "Not hurt in any way."

"I'm fine." Ella was staring at him as if she really was seeing a ghost. "How did you—"

"Carrie, the head of makeup, she said she could make me look like anyone, and I took her at her word."

Pulling off the wig and the prosthetic that had given him a blade of a nose and high, wide cheekbones, he knelt down next to the stream, pulled out the tube of cleanser Carrie had given him and started removing the makeup and bits of glue.

Ella took out her cell and flipped it open, cursed under her breath and flipped it closed again.

"No signal," she said, shoving it back in her skirt pocket. "The grandparents must be going crazy wondering what happened to me. If they saw you from a distance, who knows what they thought. You even fooled me for a moment and I was up close."

"I guess Carrie did a grand enough job for me to pass in the dim light."

Ella crouched down next to him. "But how did you know what Father looked like?"

"Internet research." Tiernan removed his shirt and used it to wipe his face clean. "I found an article about your da and printed it to read later. There was a photo of him. I gave it to Carrie."

"Whatever gave you the idea? You couldn't have known you would need to do something so drastic to rescue me."

"Indeed I could," he countered. "McKenna instinct. Or call it whatever makes you comfortable. When you wouldn't let me come with you, and so many people were so hostile, I just knew something terrible was at hand. I couldn't let anything happen to you. The ghost of your da was the only thing I could think of that would make an angry crowd hesitate long enough for me to get you out of harm's way."

"But you put yourself in danger!"

"As did you," he returned. Having stayed calm until now, Tiernan allowed himself some release. "You should have left, gone home as I suggested, but you would not."

"I *couldn't!*"

Responding to her raised voice, he tersely said, "I beg to differ! Nevertheless, when you did not, the least you could have done was taken precautions." Now that the crisis was over, he was angry with her for putting herself in jeopardy. "I offered to help you twice today and you refused."

"This was my battle to fight!"

"'Twas *our* battle, Ella. When you care for another person, you share the bad, as well as the good."

She blinked and her voice cracked. "You c-care for me?"

"Aye." Feeling his ire settle, Tiernan stroked the side of her face and thought about what Kate had said. Still, he couldn't put his true feelings into words.

She swallowed hard and dropped her gaze. "Oh."

Tiernan's breath caught in his throat. She hadn't returned the sentiment. Her confusion dashed through him like knives to his heart.

Then she looked up and said, "I was drawn to you from the first, only I didn't want to be. You were too dangerous to be around."

"I did warn you."

"I don't mean the prophecy. You were as comfortable with your psychic abilities as my father was with his...and you tried to make me use mine. *That* made me afraid of getting too close."

"Are you afraid now?"

"Right at this moment?"

"Aye."

She placed a palm on his bare chest. "How could I be after what you did for me?"

Too aware of her touching him, of his wanting to touch her, hold her, Tiernan was frozen to inaction. He wasn't frozen to her *reaction* to him, however—longing mixed with hesitation—or to his own feelings that were quickly spinning out of control.

He loved her, really loved her, something he'd never thought would happen to him. He hadn't been able to admit it to himself until he'd ridden onto the rez and had seen her in trouble. Then he had known.

His head went light with the wanting and he swayed a little closer so that his chest brushed her breasts. He felt her nipples pebble against his bare flesh and got an immediate erection. Never breaking the gaze that connected them, she ran her hand up over his neck to cup his cheek. Sweet torture, he thought, knowing he should back off.

"Oh, Tiernan," she breathed.

Just hearing his name whispered over her lips was his undoing. He had to return her touch, taste her mouth again, hold her just for a moment.

That's all it could ever be between them, he thought hazily and with remorse, as he crushed his mouth against hers.

Anything more would place her in mortal danger again, and this time he might not be able to save her.

THE STRESS OF the day melted away while in Tiernan's arms.

Though Ella knew the danger wasn't over yet and wouldn't be until they'd uncovered and stopped the villain permanently, she couldn't stop herself. Losing herself in the kiss, in the feel of his body pressed against hers, she slid her hands around his neck, scraped her nails down his back until he groaned into her mouth.

Her body quickened even before he grabbed her butt and pulled her tight against him. She couldn't get close enough to suit her, not unless she wrapped herself around him and drew him inside her.

Rocking against him, she told him what she wanted without words. And when he murmured, "Nah-nah," against her mouth and tried to push her away, she dug her nails into his back and kissed him harder. She wasn't going to let any prophecy keep them apart! He fought her for a moment, but halfheartedly, and in the end, she got her way.

Still locked in a passionate kiss, they fell to the ground, soft with pine needles, and rolled one over the other, Ella landing on top. She pulled her skirts up so that he could put his hands on her.

Seared by his fingers sliding over her cotton panties, she pushed against his hand while unbuttoning her long-sleeved blouse. She could feel his other hand, unzipping his pants, releasing himself, and the picture she had in her mind was enough to make her juices flow.

Ella reached to touch him and was gratified when Tiernan cupped her breasts and thumbed her nipples into aching peaks. Wanting to be joined with him now, she somehow managed to tear her panties away, then found him and sank slowly down his length. She gasped as every inch of her body quickened. There was a rightness to their joining. No matter what happened after—no matter the dangers they faced—they would do it together and they would prevail.

Nothing and no one could pull them apart after this.

TIERNAN AWOKE HOURS later with a weight pressed into his side. The moon was nearly full, allowing him to see Red

Crow nearby, snuffling through pine needles for something to eat. As his head cleared and his eyes focused, Tiernan realized what the weight pressing into him was.

Ella....

Then he remembered they'd spent hours making love, and according to his cell, more hours sleeping. 'Twas not so long before dawn—they had some decisions to make.

Ella was half naked, wearing only her skirt and bra and cowboy boots. He'd gotten the blouse off her, had seen the burn scars on the inside of her left arm that she carried as a reminder of what had happened to her da. She'd tried to put out the fire—such bravery and her only thirteen at the time! Tiernan could hardly believe it.

Just as he could hardly believe he'd fallen in love with Ella Thunder...or that he had acted on it!

Realizing what he'd done, Tiernan was horrified.

How could he have lost his head like that?

He'd spent most of his life vowing never to fall in love and if he fell in love never to consummate it. He'd listened to Kate and gone after Ella to fight for her.

He hadn't meant to make love to her.

Filled with guilt, he sat up, dropped his head in his hands and moaned.

"What's wrong?" came Ella's voice, still soft with sleep.

"I should not have done it," he agonized. "Should never have touched you. Now you are doomed!"

"Ohhhh...." She pushed herself up next to him. "Not the curse again."

"Why will you not believe me? You, more than anyone, know what is possible."

As she pulled on her blouse, she tried to reason with him. "I've already been in mortal danger and you saved me."

"But that was before we..." Before they'd made love. And

it *was* love, so deep that he feared it would break his heart if any harm came to Ella because of him. "You must leave. Go far from here, away from me—"

"I'm not going anywhere!"

He tried to reason with her. "I will continue the investigation without you."

"Forget it!" She got to her feet and buttoned the blouse. "Just stop being so…so…ridiculous!"

He shot to his feet next to her. "'Tis not ridiculous. If you do not go on your own, I'll—"

"What? Are you threatening me now? I didn't know macho was your style."

He looked down into her face, now as closed off from him as were her emotions. Earlier, he'd lost himself in that connection, had never felt so fulfilled, but now he simply felt…empty.

"Be reasonable, Ella. You leave and keep safe, and I promise I will find the true villain and then will come for you."

"Fine!" she spat, but he knew it was anything but.

Her anger hit him hard and so he stood there stunned as she went for Red Crow, untied his reins from the branch where they'd been fastened, then led him to a fallen limb that she apparently meant to use as a mounting block.

"What are you doing, Thunder?" he asked as she threw herself on the roan's back. "He's not saddled."

"Don't need it. You wanted me to leave, McKenna?" She reined the horse away from him. "Well, watch me leave!"

"'Tis not what I meant!" He was yelling after her, because she was already heading away from him. "You stubborn woman!"

He might as well save his breath since he was talking to himself.

Not looking forward to the walk home—headquarters was

miles away, Tiernan wondered how far he would have to go before running into a band of mustangs. Could he charm a feral horse into giving him a ride home?

He didn't know what Ella was going to do next. His biggest fear was that she would go and get herself killed and then not only would he be without her, he would have to live with that through eternity, because he would know that he was the one responsible.

ELLA SET OFF, not knowing where to go. At the moment, "nowhere" seemed safe enough. She certainly couldn't go back to the rez. And she couldn't go to refuge headquarters lest she put Kate and her family in danger.

What the heck was she going to do now?

When she left the forested area, she gave the roan his head and just rode for a while. As she rode, the horror of the night came rushing back at her.

And the beauty that had followed…

…until Tiernan had ruined it.

She tried to forget the way she'd felt in his arms, tried to hold on to the anger at his wanting to send her away. She couldn't. Regretting riding off on him and leaving him stranded, she wondered if she should turn back to find him. Well, if she *could.* Though the moon was nearly full, that didn't automatically mean she would be able to retrace her steps back to where she'd left him. If he was still there—undoubtedly he'd already left himself, and he could be anywhere between her and the refuge.

Ella pulled her cell phone from her pocket and flipped it open, the screen making a glowing blob against the night. She wanted to reassure Grandmother and Grandfather. She wanted to call Tiernan, to apologize and to see if they could figure out a way to meet up again.

She couldn't scare up a signal.

Red Crow picked his way along a path that led upward, and Ella realized she wasn't far from the mine entrance—the one Max Borland intended to blow up. In a way, that was a shame. Undoubtedly it wasn't safe, but rez kids had been climbing up there to explore and mess around for excitement for as long as she could remember. At least she assumed they still did. Though the entrance had always been boarded up, it had been easy enough to make a secret entrance, placing the loose board back in place so no one would know. Of course everyone did.

As she got closer, Ella could see the entrance was now open, free of boards, though there were wooden horses and a Do Not Enter sign. Hmm, the movie company must have been in there, rooting around, deciding where they could shoot.

Well, good for her—the mine would provide her with a safe place to hide out for a while. She could get a bit more sleep, maybe wake up with a clear vision that would tell her what to do next. Being inside the mine would certainly keep her warmer while she made plans. Even at this time of year, the mountains were cool at night, probably in the midforties, and all she was wearing was a cotton skirt and blouse. Her only warmth came from her contact with the horse.

Ella dismounted and loosely looped the reins over one of the wooden horses. A horse tied to a horse—she should at least smile at that. But the responsibility she'd taken on herself weighed her down.

What could I have done differently, Father?

If Father was listening, he wasn't answering.

Before entering the mine, she tried her cell again. Still no signal.

But the light from the cell allowed her to see what was around her as she entered the pitch-black chamber. She used it to guide her along the tracks the ore cars traveled until the tunnel split off in three directions.

Shortly after entering the left tunnel—far smaller and more claustrophobic than Ella remembered—she wanted to go back. Something stopped her from doing so. It was as if she could feel the mine itself urging her on, drawing her in deeper. The earth seemed to breathe, to expand and contract beneath her feet.

Was it her imagination, or by calling up the elements earlier to save Marisala, had she opened herself to nature's subtleties?

Feeling the earth's power like an invisible pull, she let it draw her along the tunnel and into the deep reaches of the mine where chunks of rock lay around her. Before she knew it, she was standing at another split and an opening she didn't remember.

Compelled to see what lay on the other side, she entered cautiously, her stomach squirreling and her pulse thrashing with warning. There was something here, something the earth wanted her to know. She shone her cell phone around the cavern until she noted a long, wide glint on the far wall. Moving to it, she touched the surface, felt the change in texture—ragged with smooth areas—beneath her fingers.

Shining the light from her cell on the material, she noted the metallic luster that reminded her of the rock she'd found in Marisala's trailer.

Fool's gold?

Or the real thing?

"You couldn't leave well enough alone, could you?" The voice shimmered around her.

Ella quickly turned, leading with her cell phone, but the glow fell off quickly, so she saw nothing but blurry movement in the dark.

"Someone had to stop you," she said more boldly than she was feeling.

Her mind was whirling, searching for an escape route that

didn't seem to exist. She barely remembered the tunnel system and this one not at all.

"Well, you finally found the truth you've been determined to get. I hope it's something you can live with, because you're never leaving here."

Ella didn't need to recognize the hollow voice to know who stood there.

Her stomach hollowed out and she held her breath, knowing she finally was face-to-face with the man responsible for her father's death.

Chapter Sixteen

The first thing Tiernan saw when he got back to the refuge was Red Crow munching away at grass in the pasture—of course Ella had beat him back to the house. Relief warred with his exhaustion at the difficult and lengthy hike.

He went inside to look for Ella, but she wasn't there, not in the kitchen, not in the bedroom. Nothing was amiss. No dirty clothes, no mess in the bath to indicate she had been there. She hadn't left because her things were still spread out on the dresser and her case was still tucked into the closet along with her clothes.

"Kate?" he called.

No answer. Everyone was out of the house.

He tried Ella's cell, but all he got for his trouble was her voice mail. His jaw clenched all through her cheery greeting as he waited to leave a message.

"Ella, be angry with me if you must, but please call me and let me know you are safe."

An exhausted Tiernan took a quick shower and put on fresh clothes. He desperately could use a lie down, but he couldn't rest until he knew Ella was unharmed.

Where could she be? Surely she hadn't gone back to the reservation....

Which is exactly what Tiernan feared.

Perhaps Ella had gone to look for Nathan again—she had told him that she had never found her cousin the night before. Or perhaps she'd just gone to check on her grandparents, to make sure *they* had not been harmed.

Whatever reason she might have to return to the reservation, she would be giving the people who might have killed her a second chance to do so.

There was only one thing for it, then, Tiernan thought. He had to go after her. The truck was on the set, so he saddled Red Crow.

"Sorry, lad. I know you were ridden hard yesterday, but you've had more rest than I, and I need to find Ella as swiftly as possible."

Riding a horse wasn't all that swift, but it gave him a flexibility that a vehicle couldn't. He didn't have to follow the roads, and a comfortable trot would take him to the reservation in less than half an hour. On the way, he tried to stay in a positive frame of mind. Even if Ella *was* there on the reservation, she would be all right. Perhaps she wasn't answering her cell because she'd run out of battery.

When he arrived at her grandparent's house, he tied up Red Crow in the shade of an elm tree. Before he could even reach the front door, it flew open. Ella's grandmother, Dina, grabbed his arm and rushed him in, then peered out the doorway as if expecting he'd been followed.

"We don't know where Ella is," she said, exchanging significant glances with her husband, who came out of the kitchen to join them.

Worry pulsated from both elderly people. While they appeared exhausted, as if they hadn't slept all night, Marisala Saldana serenely sat in a rocking chair by the window. Humming under her breath, she was lost in her own head, not even seeming to notice his presence. Indeed, though he tested her, he got nothing but confused thoughts and images.

Ella's grandfather said, "Someone rescued Ella from an angry crowd last night...."

"I'm the one who rescued her with the help of a makeup artist," Tiernan admitted. He wasn't about to detail the way they'd connected, so he skipped to the important part. "Later, we fought. I wanted Ella to leave, to go someplace safe. She was angry with me. She took the horse and headed off. I fear for her safety, for I do not know where she went...and she has not contacted me since."

"We tried to find out what happened to our granddaughter." Samuel Thunder sat down hard as if he couldn't control his ire. "Jimmy Iron Horse was no help!"

Dina Thunder cast forth both dread and anger. "We went to him, demanded he find Ella and protect her, and he told me that if she turned herself in, he would be glad to help. As if *she* was the one who had done something wrong."

"A shame on The People," Samuel muttered. "They took our son from us, and now they want to take our granddaughter. I am ashamed to call the rez our home. When you find Ella, do whatever you must to get her away from this place. We should have left years ago when our son was taken from us, but even then we were too old and without resources to start over." He mourned. "If we had gone then, Ella would never have had a reason to come back to this cursed place!"

Tiernan's heart went out to the couple. "I can try to convince her again, but as I am sure you know, Ella is very strong-willed. And she blames what happened only on one man—the sorcerer who put fear in the hearts and confusion in the minds of your people. She is determined to find and stop him before he can do any more harm."

The grandparents gave each other a significant look, then Dina said, "Her father wouldn't use his power to fight for himself, and I do not think Ella will, either. You must convince her to do whatever she must to protect herself...or to leave forever. We would rather lose her to the white world than see her die. That would break our hearts all over again."

"Can you think of anywhere I might look?" Tiernan asked. "Or anyone I might speak with who could help?"

"Our grandson Nathan will help you find Ella and protect her," Samuel said. "Go to him."

Tiernan didn't argue. Let them believe what they would. Though he didn't expect help from Nathan, he wanted to see the man anyway. If Ella's cousin was the guilty one, he would know soon enough. Her grandparents could wait for the bad news until he was certain.

"Would you know where I might find Nathan?" he asked. "Ella was looking for him yesterday but never found him."

"He has a cabin out of town halfway to the top of the mountain. Perhaps he went there," Samuel said, then gave directions on how to find it.

Tiernan thanked them and was about to leave when Marisala suddenly awakened from her stupor.

"*He* took Ella," she muttered darkly, her eyes unnaturally wide and bright. "He stole Ella Thunder and won't give her back. With Ella out of the way, he'll be able to do whatever he wants to any of us. No one can stop him now."

"He...who?"

Did she mean Nathan or not? He didn't ask, not wanting the elderly couple upset if it wasn't necessary.

Tiernan's hopes that Marisala would clarify were soon dashed, for she quickly became lost in her own world again. He could feel her spirit retreat and her mind lose focus. He thanked the Thunders and promised he would let them know when he found their granddaughter. Waves of hope warring with fear washed over him as he left the house.

Once out of town, he turned Red Crow onto the gravel road and pulled out his cell to call Kate. He was relieved when she answered on the second ring.

"I'm off in search of Ella, Kate. After she brought Red Crow back, she simply disappeared."

"Ella didn't bring back Red Crow, Tiernan. He found his way home on his own. When I left the house at dawn, he was wandering outside. I fed and watered him and then put him in the pasture myself." Kate heaved a worried-sounding sigh, yet said, "Tiernan…I—I'm sure she's fine."

He couldn't shake the sense of doom that hung over his head. "'Tis the prophecy, Kate."

"Then fight for her, Tiernan. Don't give up. It's not too late. It can't be."

He couldn't keep thinking about it. If he did, he would be lost, unable to do what he must so that he could save the woman he loved.

Twenty minutes later, having taken the road higher into the mountains to a small log cabin, he tied Red Crow to a hitching post with a trough where the horse could get water. Before he could approach the cabin, the front door opened and Nathan stood there, silent, staring at Tiernan as if he could see right through him.

"What is it you want, McKenna?" Nathan asked.

Tiernan didn't stop until he was directly in front of the man. The closer he got, the better chance he had of reading him. Of knowing the truth. "I am looking for Ella."

"Ella's not here."

When Nathan easily blocked him from getting anything off him, Tiernan bit down his frustration. He needed to feel, as well as hear, what Nathan Lantero had to say in order to know the truth.

"Where is she, then?"

"How would I know?"

"She's your cousin."

Nathan dipped his head in agreement. "We are related...but I hardly know her anymore."

"You saved her from burning to death once."

"In another lifetime."

"Are you not concerned at what happens to someone you once cared about?"

Nathan let down his guard for a moment and the rush of regret that wrapped around Tiernan put him on edge.

"As hard as it might be for you to believe, I still care about her," Nathan said. "What is it you want from me?"

"I already told you."

"Yes, you're looking for Ella, but there's something more. Something darker."

Was Nathan reading him? He seemed to be in tune with Tiernan's fears.

"There's Marisala."

Nathan started. "What about her?"

"Something happened to her. Something bad." The rush of panic suddenly enveloping Tiernan made him realize Nathan had just lost control. Good, then he would get to the truth. "Marisala is gone, Nathan. She's a shell. Out of her mind. Someone did that to her purposely and with malice. The question is—was it you?"

"I would never hurt Marisala!"

The sense of shock and disbelief whirling around them almost convinced Tiernan, but he had to be certain.

"You're not wearing your buffalo totem," he said. When Nathan didn't answer, Tiernan filled him in. "Yesterday morning, Ella found Marisala out of her mind and took her to the reservation clinic for observation. Afterward, we went back to her trailer to see if we could figure out who did this to her, and we found your totem."

"I must have left it there when I was with her a couple nights ago. I would never hurt Marisala," Nathan repeated. "Because I *love* her. She swore she loved me, too, but she wanted off this rez and I finally found where I belong—right here!—and I wouldn't leave again, not even for her. I wasn't enough for her, couldn't offer her enough, so she told me she found someone else. Obviously someone dangerous." He shook his head. "Where is she now?"

"With your grandparents."

Nathan slammed the door behind him and started to push by Tiernan. "I must go to her."

Tiernan put out an arm and stopped him. "For now, Marisala is safe. Ella…I am not so confident."

"How long has she been missing?"

"We were together last night, but we fought, and she went off alone. Something happened to her." Then he faced the truth. Warped mind and all, Marisala had been spot on. "The villain took Ella…stole her," he said, remembering Marisala's words. "He has her now. If she was safe, she would never let us all worry like this."

"She would have called someone," Nathan agreed.

"How the hell will I ever find her?"

"If she is aware, she can find you."

Startled by that, Tiernan echoed, "Aware? What do you mean?"

"On another plane. If she were to call on the abilities she inherited from her father—"

"Which she is afraid to use."

"If she were to journey, and if you were receptive…open to it…"

Tiernan remembered Ella saying that, of all her da's apprentices, Nathan had held the most promise. "She told me *you* had abilities, as well. Why can't you use them to find her?"

Nathan shook his head. "I gave up the Lakota mysticism I practiced to fit in with the white world. While I still walk a more aware path than the majority of The People…I can no longer do this or I would."

If he wasn't lying through his teeth, Tiernan thought, though he got nothing from the man that would tell him otherwise.

And then Nathan said, "Perhaps you can find Ella yourself," which made Tiernan's heart skip a beat.

"What makes you think that?"

"I can still sense power in a man," Nathan said. "I sense something in you. Besides, you're the one with a connection to Ella. If that connection is strong enough, you will be able to reach her."

Tiernan tried to get a handle on what Nathan was saying. Reach her how? On this other plane? Before he could settle it in his mind, Nathan pushed by him, so determined to go after Marisala that Tiernan didn't try to stop him.

As Nathan got into his truck, he called out, "I hope you find her in time."

"In time?"

But the sound of the truck's door slamming drowned out his question. Nathan took off and Tiernan ran for Red Crow.

In time…

The clock was ticking.

COLD SEEPED THROUGH her thin cotton clothing and enveloped her flesh, making Ella wonder why she had ever thought the mine would keep her warm. She'd been fine when she'd been moving through the tunnels searching for answers, but now that she was tied up and on the ground, a cool stream of air blowing over her, she was chilled straight through.

To make it worse, her head ached and every time she tried to lift it, she felt the tunnel whirl around her. Before she had been able to identify the villain, there'd been a loud crack and a flash of light, after which she'd felt a sharp pain in her thigh. Then she'd dropped to the tunnel floor.

Another dart, she assumed.

Though she worked at the bindings keeping her hands behind her back, she made no headway at removing them. Her feet were secured, as well, and the two sets of rope were attached one to the other, so she couldn't even stand and try to hop out of there. She lay on her side in a soft arc.

How long had it been?

Was it day or night?

What was he planning on doing to her?

As if she'd sent some kind of signal that she was awake, footsteps echoed down the tunnel toward her. She rolled over so she could see in that direction and realized the man was carrying a battery-powered lantern in such a way that she still couldn't see his face.

Would he continue to hide his identity from her?

Not if she could help it.

Tuning in to her higher self, Ella quickly grew aware. She analyzed every sound and movement the villain made, and when he stopped, the lantern held out before him illuminating her and the surrounding area and little else—certainly not him—it no longer mattered.

"Afraid of me?" she asked. Maybe he should be—even she didn't know what she might be able to do once her head cleared of the drug. For now, however, she subdued the anger that seethed inside her—she needed answers first. "Maybe you should be afraid."

"Big talk for someone who is in my power." He disguised his voice with a low, raspy tone.

"So why haven't you killed me?"

"I don't need to," he said, laughing. "The mine will do it for me."

Just as she'd thought—he didn't want to do the dirty work himself. He would just as soon leave her to die of thirst and then let her rot.

"And yet you had to come to check on me, to make sure I was still here," she said.

"You're not going anywhere. And I'm not here for you. I have work to do."

She analyzed the way he spoke, the cadence and intonation. And promptly eliminated one of the three suspects. "Need more gold?"

"So…you figured it out."

"Kind of hard not to after seeing that vein. I made the mistake of assuming the rock I found in Marisala's trailer was fool's gold."

"Marisala was a greedy bitch!"

He nearly lost it, she thought, nearly gave up the altered voice.

She asked, "Is that why you took Marisala's mind?"

His harsh laughter filled the tunnel. "She stopped being interesting and fun and became a problem."

"Which you never liked dealing with, did you, Leonard?" she asked, now certain of the villain's identity. "You might as well step into the light, let me see the man responsible for my death."

"How did you know?" Leonard Hawkins asked, now in his normal voice.

"If I hadn't already sensed you, the conversation would

have done it. You always did shy away from dealing with anything that was too difficult."

"You wouldn't believe the things I've done."

"Like set up my father? I didn't know you had it in you, Leonard—the abilities, I mean. But what did Father ever do to you?"

"Joseph interfered with my plans. He discovered my secret—the gold I'd found and sold. He said it belonged to the tribe, that I couldn't keep it for myself even if I was the one who spent years looking for it. And when I did make that first strike, it wasn't like I was able to get a fortune out. I was only using the old tools. It was barely enough to give me a better life."

"But apparently, you improved your skills. Then you made sure the casino was approved and built and demanded to run it. Great cover. No one would question why you had so much more than anyone else. Did you ever think that if there was a concerted effort by the tribe to remove the gold from this mine, there would be enough money for everyone to have a better life?"

"I couldn't let them in here. They would have ruined everything."

She didn't know if it was the confusion caused by the drug or if he was being purposely cryptic. "I don't get it."

"The *Paha Sapa* gives me my powers."

Her father had made the same claim. "What does that have to do with the mine?"

"I need to be *inside* the mountain. I developed my powers in *here* when I was messing around one day. And this is the only place I can use them effectively."

Leonard was so superstitious that he believed he could only journey in this specific mine, Ella realized.

"The reason you never left the rez."

Sounding angry, he said, "Now the movie company will invade the mine—"

"And you're afraid they will find your gold."

"They plan to blow up the entrance. Not only would I lose the gold—"

"You would lose your power," Ella finished for him.

She wondered if he'd considered the caves. There were a couple on rez land that would bring him inside the mountain just as well as did this mine. Not that she was going to give him any ideas.

"Enough! I have work to do!" Leonard picked up his lantern and walked past her.

Ella rolled to watch him as he approached another branch and, circling what looked to be a mine shaft that would take him even deeper in the mountain, chose the left tunnel.

At least she knew who and why. Now all she had to do was figure out how to free herself.

And how to bring him down.

If only she didn't have to face this alone....

If only she hadn't let her temper best her and make her leave Tiernan, she wouldn't be in this fix.

Or they would be in it together.

Together...as they should be. She'd felt the connection all along, but she'd wanted to deny it. No longer. If only he were here. If only she could do something to let Tiernan know where she was.

A thrill shot through her as she realized that maybe she *could* let him know.

If the mine had truly augmented Leonard's powers, maybe it would do the same for her.

Closing her eyes, Ella focused, sought help from the elements. The air current circled her and the tunnel floor below her began to gently vibrate.

Give me the ability to reach the man I love.

You have it in you, Ella, her father says. You always have. It's time.

The journey? she asked.

Your other half will make you whole.

Her other half…Tiernan. *She focused inward, drew on her memory of him the last time she saw him.*

I'm sorry, Tiernan. I never should have left like I did. Hear me. Please.

She hurtled through the clouds, and propelled by the wind, she sought him in every direction.

Tiernan, I need you! she called.

The air shifted and she slowed and her surroundings came into focus. She was in a stand of ponderosa pines like the ones where they'd lain together the night before. She felt his essence and followed the trail, eventually catching sight of him, straight-spined and determined, riding one with Red Crow.

Tiernan, please find me before it's too late….

Chapter Seventeen

Having found the place where they'd spent half the night, Tiernan moved Red Crow in the same direction Ella had taken. Not knowing how far she had gone before separating from the horse, he kept an eagle eye on the surroundings—every spruce, every poplar, every juniper, and all the rocks and crags between and behind them—even as he came up with an alternate plan.

Two Lakota had said they recognized his power—Nathan, and before him, Bear Heart. Had they seen something in him that went beyond what he'd experienced? How could he stretch himself to find Ella before it was too late?

Too stressed to figure it all out, he decided to use what he knew he had in his psychic arsenal.

"Whoa, lad," he murmured, bringing Red Crow to a stop. Patting the gelding's neck, he hopped off and moved around so they were face-to-face. "I need you to show me where you took Ella," he murmured.

A simple parlor trick, he could connect with the recent past experienced by his subject, the way he'd known Ella had been hit by a dart that first day.

Pulling the gelding's head down, he touched him, forehead to forehead, then reached out with his mind, forcing an image of their night's camp to the beast. After which, he replayed Ella mounting the horse bareback and their taking off down a trail away from him.

"C'mon, Red Crow, keep going…."

He mentally replayed the images like a loop, Ella leaving him over and over again, going down the same trail, him urging the horse to retrace his steps.

As if he suddenly realized what the human wanted of him, Red Crow snorted and bobbed his head, smacking Tiernan's so that stars danced in his mind.

Then the stars faded….

The surroundings bobbed…distorted…trees and boulders of increasing size…jagged rocky peaks that creepily moved closer…

"Yes, that's it, good lad!"

Having recognized the direction he needed to take, Tiernan patted the gelding and stepped into the saddle. Before he could seat himself, Red Crow was off.

Tiernan gave the roan his head.

The horse picked his way out of the forested area and onto a trail that took them upward—Tiernan assumed in the direction he'd taken Ella earlier.

Still connected with Red Crow, he filled the horse's mind with images of Ella, hoping that would keep the beast going in the correct direction, one that would bring him to the woman herself. He looked around, saw the same scenery, those same peaks he had when he'd done that mind meld trick.

Up…up…up they went….

The higher they went, the more separated Tiernan felt from the reality of where they were. Drifting rudderless, he swore he could feel Ella, could almost hear her calling his name.

Perhaps she was…

He closed his eyes.

Ella? Are you there?

Suddenly feeling lost in a vacuum, Tiernan panicked and, his heart thumping, flashed open his eyes. Red Crow stopped as if waiting for directions. Where to go? Nothing but trees and brush and rock around.

And the mine.

Tiernan sat there for a moment, staring at the entrance, seeking the link with Ella that had been faint but was now lost. He had to find it again. Had to find *her.*

Closing his eyes, he freed his mind, sent it searching. He had no focus, no direction. He was testing something intangible. Trusting that others saw in him some truth he did not even know he possessed, he gave himself up to a hope he'd never before had.

He was seeking an indefinable connection that would bring Ella and him together in the most intimate way of all, only as those who loved each other could do.

He couldn't lose her, not now. He had to fight for her in any way he could.

Ella, are you there?

No response. His pulse threaded unevenly as he tried again.

Ella, where are you?

Still nothing. Tiernan forced his mind to reach further than ever before....

And then he felt her.

Ella!

Find me, Tiernan, before it's too late!

Where are you?

Open your mind and you'll see....

Tiernan was more than willing to do as Ella asked. At least he hoped it was Ella. Hoped he hadn't fabricated her voice because he needed to hear it. He wanted to open his mind as she asked, only he didn't know how.

Dismounting, he fastened the reins around a bush branch and moved toward the mine entrance. At the mouth, he went inside and touched the tunnel walls. Then he closed his eyes and tried to get from the inanimate rock what he'd gotten from the very much alive Red Crow. He'd never tried this before, didn't know if it would work, but he sensed Ella had been here.

Ella and someone else, someone intent on evil.

After taking a good look down the tunnel as far as the light went, he closed his eyes.

Rock cool against his palms, Tiernan concentrated on the tunnel itself, attempting to link himself to any lingering memory here—hoping it would give him a road map that could lead him to his woman. He moved slowly, through light into shadow and crossed over into the dark. He imagined Ella doing the same.

His inner vision was suddenly lit with a weird bluish glow.

Light from a cell phone?

Must be.

Ella! he called, mentally beseeching her to appear so that he could be certain.

He followed the light through a maze of tunnels, keeping track of every twist and turn of direction. Feeling the earth's power like an invisible pull, he let it draw him into the deep reaches of the mine. Suddenly he paused at another split, unsure of which route to take.

Which way, Ella, which way?

An invisible hand drew him to the left. He entered cautiously, anticipation jackhammering through him. He felt her. She was close. Had to be. The glow shone around the cavern to a thready glint on the far wall. But as he moved to it, something made him stop and refocus downward.

She lay arched in a soft bow, her hands and feet behind her. Groggily, she opened her eyes and he bent down to release her. She shook her head.

Hurry...find me...or it'll be too late....

It cannot be. I am responsible for this.

No! she cried.

I love you. I should have—

And I love you, Tiernan. Fight for me!

The vision fading, Tiernan gasped and his eyes flew open. First he would have to find her. Nathan had been right. He'd just had some kind of out-of-body journey.

Before forgetting one minutiae of the vision, he ran back to the horse, calling Kate on his cell as he did so. Listening to her voice-mail message, he pulled a flashlight and a first-aid kit from the saddle bag. Attaching them to his belt, he left an S.O.S.—surely Kate would check her messages in time.

"Kate, I need backup and fast! I'm at the old mine on the reservation, the entrance the movie company is going to blow up. Ella is in there. I have to get to her!"

As he flipped the cell closed, he was already hurrying to the mine entrance and praying he wouldn't be too late to save Ella.

Tick-tock.

How long did he have?

THOROUGHLY DEPLETED, ELLA lay there with the cold shutting down first her body, then her mind, praying with everything she had left that Tiernan could find her. He was so close, she could almost feel him.

If he didn't find her soon, he would be too late. The cold beckoned sleep, and she was having a difficult time fighting to stay awake. Some part of her heard Tiernan calling her with renewed urgency, but rescue seemed so elusive....

Leonard—where was he? She hadn't heard him hack away at the ore in the tunnel in a while. For all she knew, he could have walked right by her and left the mine. Or gotten lost in it.

Something in her wanted to laugh at the thought. How

would Leonard Hawkins feel if he were to be forever trapped in the mine that gave him his money and power?

What irony that would be.

Footsteps, faint at first, then louder, warned her someone drew near. She shook her head to clear it and bit the inside of her lip to wake herself.

"Ella!"

The sound of his voice rushed toward her along with a light so bright it at first hurt her eyes. Her chest opened, allowing her to breathe again, and she felt as if her heart were exposed.

"Tiernan!"

"I have you now," he said, pulling the knife from the sheath at his waist and reaching over her to get at the rope binding her feet to her hands.

A sharp tug from him and suddenly she was half-freed, able to lower her legs. What she could still feel of them. Then he was cutting away the ties securing her wrists—she felt the rope fall away from them—and then he freed her feet.

Tiernan's hands on her as he helped her into a sitting position had never felt so good. Somehow she threw her half-lifeless arms around his neck.

"I can't believe you found me, Tiernan. I thought this was the end of me."

"What makes you think it isn't?"

The caustic question echoed from somewhere behind them. Even as Tiernan lifted her onto her feet, Ella glanced back to see Leonard coming down the tunnel toward them. He was still far enough away that they could escape…they had to after the way she and Tiernan had finally connected. They couldn't lose each other now!

"We have to get out of here," she choked out, her throat as dry as parchment.

Her limbs were still stiff and unmanageable, so Tiernan

half carried her back the way he'd come. His very touch filled her with longing. And with hope that they would get out of this alive and together.

"You don't think I'll let you leave so easily," came the warning from much closer behind them.

Ella glanced back but this time there was no light. Leonard had been wandering these tunnels for decades, so he could no doubt navigate them in the dark. He could be right behind them and they wouldn't know it until it was too late.

"We have to get out now before he finds us." Ella pushed herself to go faster. "He gets his power from being inside the mountain. He could be anywhere, do anything to us."

When she shuddered against him, Tiernan held her tighter. "I can fight him. I must be able to fight him. I will not lose you."

Ella knew he was thinking about the family curse and finally conceded there might be a reason to suggest that his worry was valid. Life was coming back into her limbs and they were functioning better, plus she was fully awake and feeling stronger. She had to find a way out of this…couldn't give up now.

"Leonard is able to affect minds—people and animals both," Ella said, thinking of the horses that had appeared to be sick. "But I'm not convinced that he can go beyond that, and I don't believe Leonard can affect *our* minds the way he has others. He wasn't able to sway Nathan the day my father was killed," she remembered. "Maybe that's because Nathan had power of his own. As do *we*."

"*You* have the power."

"You're the one who figured out how to find me, Tiernan, so I'm not alone. It's time that you admitted you're not without power yourself."

"Being psychic isn't the same thing as being able to make things happen," he argued. "And, by the way, my psychic powers tell me we have company."

Tiernan spun around and aimed his flashlight. A few yards behind them, Leonard put a hand up to his face to protect his eyes, then tossed his lantern at Tiernan's arm. Direct hit. Both lights went flying in opposite directions, and Ella could feel Leonard trying to force his will on Tiernan.

Fighting back her fear, Ella mentally sought the plane that remained just out of her reach. She hadn't felt as if she could use her inherited powers on herself, but she had saved Marisala and she would do everything in her power to save the man she loved!

Tiernan's body seemed to obey Leonard. He jerked like a marionette as he struggled against getting down on his knees, but he was fighting a losing battle.

Rather than beseeching Father for help, Ella opened her mind and let it race along a higher plane, one Father had taught her to reach so many years ago. A light wind began whirling around her body and the earth started trembling beneath her feet. Her calling up the elements in her mind felt easier—more natural—to her this time.

Concentrating on a softball-sized piece of loose rock in one corner of the tunnel, she imagined it moving…lifting…flying at Leonard and knocking him off balance.

Just that quickly, the rock hit him in reality.

His concentration broken, Leonard had no choice but to mentally release Tiernan, who went after him physically full force. The men's bodies exploded back down the tunnel the way they'd just come. Her heart in her throat, Ella went for the discarded lantern, and turning the light on the men, took in an angry McKenna in action. His fists moved so fast, Leonard didn't have time to duck. Tiernan hit him over and over, driving him farther back in the mine.

Realizing he might be forcing Leonard to a place of even more power, she cried, "No. *No!* Tiernan, let him be. Let's get out of here now while we can!"

But Tiernan either didn't hear her or was ignoring her. And Leonard was suddenly giving as good as he got. Now it was Tiernan who bashed into a tunnel wall, Leonard who went after him, pummeling his face bloody.

Rushing after them, Ella thought fast. How was she going to stop them? Stop Leonard from killing Tiernan and then her? After this, Leonard wasn't simply going to trust their deaths to the mine—he would put an end to them for sure.

Fear and loathing whirling inside her, Ella felt her skirts flutter around her legs and then rise eerily around her. She felt as if she was electrically charged…her mind spinning out of control.

Before her, Tiernan caught on to Leonard and the men danced down the tunnel together, slipping and bouncing off walls and crashing to the floor and sliding farther away from her. Her gaze whipped beyond them to the mine shaft! Her chest tightened as she imagined Leonard tossing Tiernan down there like so much garbage.

The men separated and backed off and Ella could see that Leonard had a grip on Tiernan's mind once more. While Tiernan thrashed and made unintelligible sounds, he couldn't get control of his body, couldn't get back to his feet. Suddenly his hands shot to his head and his yell of agony echoed down the tunnel, engulfing her.

Fearing Leonard was doing to Tiernan what he had done to Marisala, Ella acted without thinking. The rock beneath Leonard's feet quaked, and a soughing wind shot down the tunnel, straight at him.

Leonard tried to summon his own power to fight her, but he wasn't fast enough. The wind pushed-pushed-pushed at him. Tripping over his own feet, he stumbled farther into the reaches of the mine, toward the waiting arms of the shaft. Ella didn't let up until he teetered on the precipice.

Leonard screamed as he lost his balance. Arms and legs flailing, he held himself in suspended animation above the opening for a moment.

Ella wouldn't let go of the vision she'd conjured and, his face a mask of terror, Leonard finally caved and fell. Before her amazed eyes, Ella saw rocks of every shape and size follow. Chunks from all directions flew to the shaft and tumbled in, just as if a magnet had drawn them there.

The mountain that had obsessed him buried Leonard.

Ella gasped and mentally let go.

Now he would be one with it forever.

Chapter Eighteen

Leonard's death scream echoed along the tunnel walls as Tiernan watched the wound in the rock floor close. An illusion? he wondered. He squeezed his eyes shut and took another look. No, the shaft really was gone and the threat with it.

"Leonard should be happy," Tiernan said. "Now he's *part* of the mountain."

He looked to Ella who was shaking—whether from fear and stress or from sheer exhaustion, he couldn't tell. Swiftly moving to her side, he slid his arms around her and held her close to his heart. A cry escaping her, she clung to him as if she couldn't believe she was touching him.

"We did it, Tiernan! We're both still alive. You fought for me and you won! You broke the curse!"

He only hoped she was correct. "We both fought for each other. 'Twas you who saved *my* life."

"Which only proves we're meant to be together."

"So it does...."

His words dissipated in her mouth, because he was kissing her as if his life depended on it. Or rather his happiness. They had bested the curse together, and they could have a future he'd never believed possible.

When he broke the kiss and pressed his forehead to hers, Ella asked, "What now? Who do we tell?

"Tell what?" Tiernan looked to the mine's floor that was worn as smooth as if there never had been an open shaft. "I see nothing to tell."

Ella moved to where Leonard had vanished. "I feel nothing. It's as if he never existed. But the tribe has a right to know the truth. Otherwise, The People will still be looking to *me* as the one who brought evil back to the rez."

Realizing she had a point, he took her hand and pulled her away from the death site, toward the outside and the light of day. He had the woman he loved for a moment, but the terror of McKenna history when it came to love still plagued him, and he wasn't absolutely certain Ella was out of danger yet.

"Will the members of the tribe believe you if you give them the truth, then?"

"I can't be sure. If only Marisala was in her right mind…"

"Perhaps Nathan can get the truth from her."

"Nathan?"

"I faced him down when I was searching for you," Tiernan told her. "Doing so convinced me he was not the one who took you. When he heard about Marisala…I felt everything he did. He loves the woman, Ella. He went after her to see that she was all right."

He felt relief shudder through her.

"Then I will trust my cousin to believe me…and to find a way to convince The People. There's also the gold here. The tribe has a right to know it exists. My father wanted Leonard to tell them about it."

"The reason Leonard set out to destroy him."

"Exactly. Tiernan, from the vein of gold I saw, there could be enough to make at least some difference in all their lives."

Snugging Ella to his side, Tiernan loved her for her

concern…added to all the other reasons. He wondered, though, if the tribe would take and sell the ore from the mountain, considering they had not taken the money awarded by the government for the land itself. Would this present a conflict of interest for them?

Even as they exited the mine, a truck and an SUV roared up the road. Tension sucked the joy from Tiernan for a moment, until he realized Kate had brought the troops. She and Chase alighted from the SUV and Nathan jumped out of the truck.

"Thank God the two of you are all right!" Kate cried, hugging both Tiernan and Ella at once.

Tiernan hugged his cousin in return, but his focus was on the woman who'd followed Nathan—Marisala stood back, staring at them with wide, clear eyes.

"Nathan?" Ella said, looking from him to the other woman.

"He brought me to protect me," said a very aware-sounding Marisala.

"I do not understand." Tiernan could hardly believe that Marisala was herself again. "How is this possible?"

"The magic died with Leonard," Ella explained. "Anything he corrupted should revert to the way it was."

"I'm so sorry," Marisala said, hanging her head. "I was selfish. Wrong. When I realized what Leonard was, I should have warned everyone."

"If anyone would have believed you then," Ella said.

"They will now," Nathan predicted. "Now with Leonard gone, everyone will believe the truth."

AS NATHAN PREDICTED, Marisala wasn't the only one relieved of Leonard's influence. Ella was happy to see the woman was trying to make up her betrayal to Nathan, and because her cousin loved the woman, he forgave her. But those who had contributed to Ella's father's death and had almost caused her own were ashamed, as well.

Most of them, anyway.

Now that they knew the secret of the mountain, The People were at odds about whether or not to reopen the mine. Just in case, Nathan had gotten an injunction against the movie company from blowing up the entrance.

Thinking about all that had happened, Ella knew she should leave and be done with the rez. Only she didn't want to. The grandparents needed her. The People needed her. Most of all, Tiernan needed her and she needed him. She'd been afraid he was too much like her own father—now she was glad that he was. If he hadn't used his psychic vision, if he hadn't tuned into hers, she might be dead now. The prophecy made against his ancestor might have come true again.

Since the rescue, they'd been together every moment possible, Tiernan always watching her as if fearing he might lose her at any time. He'd been careful *not* to bring up the future.

A few days had passed since they'd overcome Leonard.

Having finished their work on the set for the week, they rode up into the hills at sunset. Ella had never felt so at ease, so happy, and from the way Tiernan kept smiling at her, she guessed he felt the same. Maybe he was finally relaxing, finally admitting they'd overcome the prophecy that had for so long guided his personal life.

They dismounted, secured the horses and sat on a ridge overlooking a pasture dotted with a herd of feral mustangs. The red ball of sun was touching the peaks on the opposite side of the valley, and Ella thought she'd never seen anything so beautiful. And with Tiernan's arm around her, she'd never been so content.

"I've made a decision," she told him.

"And what might that be?"

"I'm not returning to Sioux Falls. I'm going to stay right here where people need me."

A smile lit his still bruised face. "I hope you include me."

"Especially you. I'm going to teach at the rez school, but Grandmother wants me to do more. To follow in Father's footsteps."

"What do *you* want?"

"I haven't decided yet. About being a shaman, that is. I do want to be with you…if you plan to stay, as well, after the movie is finished shooting." She held her breath waiting for the answer.

"I have been thinking on it," Tiernan admitted. "I love the country…the people…" He gave her a sappy look on that one. "And horses. Cows not so much. I was considering buying a small spread and starting a business, breeding and training horses."

"Thoroughbreds?"

"Or quarter horses. I haven't thought it through that far yet."

"Then you're staying, too!" she said, happiness soaring through her.

"'Tis the only way I can have the woman I love. A huge sacrifice, but one I'm willing to make."

He winked at her, and she giggled and the next thing she knew she was in his arms having the breath kissed right out of her.

The sun dipped below the peaks opposite sending streaks of red in every direction…the landscape turning as bright and warm as their future together promised to be.

* * * * *

RICK'S APPOINTMENT with his attorney early Wednesday morning went only moderately better than his meeting with social services the day before. The prognosis wasn't great—but at least his attorney was going to file a motion for DNA testing. Just so Rick could petition to see the child…his sister's baby. The sister he didn't know he had until it was too late.

The rest of what his attorney said had been downhill from there.

Cell phone in hand before he'd even reached his Nitro, Rick punched in the speed-dial number he'd programmed the day before.

Maybe foster parent Sue Bookman hadn't received his message. Or had lost his number. Maybe she didn't want to talk to him. At this point he didn't much care what she wanted.

"Hello?" She answered before the first ring was complete. And sounded breathless.

Young and breathless.

"Ms. Bookman?"

"Yes. This is Rick Kraynick, right?"

"Yes, ma'am."

"I recognized your number on caller ID," she said, her voice uneven, as though she was still engaged in whatever physical activity had her so breathless to begin with. "I'm sorry I didn't get back to you. I've been a little…distracted."

The words came in more disjointed spurts. Was she jogging?

"No problem," he said, when, in fact, he'd spent the better part of the night before watching his phone. And fretting. "Did I get you at a bad time?"

"No worse than usual," she said, adding, "Better than some. So, how can I help?"

God, if only this could be so easy. He'd ask. She'd help. And life could go well. At least for one little person in his family.

It would be a first.

"Mr. Kraynick?"

"Yes. Sorry. I was… Are you sure there isn't a better time to call?"

"I'm bouncing a baby, Mr. Kraynick. It's what I do."

"Is it Carrie?" he asked quickly, his pulse racing.

"How do you know Carrie?" She sounded defensive, which wouldn't do him any good.

"I'm her uncle," he explained, "her mother's—Christy's—older brother, and I know you have her."

"I can neither confirm nor deny your allegations, Mr. Kraynick. Please call social services." She rattled off the number.

"Wait!" he said, unable to hide his urgency. "Please," he said more calmly. "Just hear me out."

"How did you find me?"

"A friend of Christy's."

"I'm sorry I can't help you, Mr. Kraynick," she said softly. "This conversation is over."

"I grew up in foster care," he said, as though that gave him some special privilege. Some insider's edge.

"Then you know you shouldn't be calling me at all."

"Yes… But Carrie is my niece," he said. "I need to see her. To know that she's okay."

"You'll have to go through social services to arrange that."

"I'm sure you know it's not as easy as it sounds. I'm a single man with no real ties and I've no intention of petitioning for custody. They aren't real eager to give me the time of day. I never even knew Carrie's mother. For all intents and purposes, our mother didn't raise either one of us. All I have going for me is half a set of genes. My lawyer's on it, but it could be weeks—months—before this is sorted out. Carrie could be adopted by then. Which would be fine, great for her, but then I'd have lost my chance. I don't want to take her. I won't hurt her. I just have to see her."

"I'm sorry, Mr. Kraynick, but…"

* * * * *

Find out if Rick Kraynick will ever have a chance to meet his niece.

Look for A DAUGHTER'S TRUST by Tara Taylor Quinn, available in September 2009.

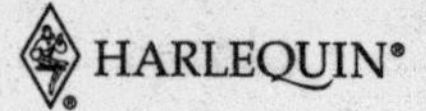

INTRIGUE®

COMING NEXT MONTH

Available September 8, 2009

#1155 SMOKIN' SIX-SHOOTER by B.J. Daniels
Whitehorse, Montana: The Corbetts
Although her new neighbor is all cowboy, she isn't looking for love—she wants answers to an unsolved murder. But when she digs too deep and invites the attention of a killer, her cowboy may be all that stands between her and a certain death.

#1156 AN UNEXPECTED CLUE by Elle James
Kenner County Crime Unit
When his cover is blown, the undercover FBI agent fears for the life of his wife and the child she carries. Although she no longer trusts him, he'll do whatever he has to do to save her and win back her love.

#1157 HIS SECRET LIFE by Debra Webb
Colby Agency: Elite Reconnaissance Division
Her mission is to find a hero who doesn't want to be found, but this Colby Agency P.I. always gets her man. She just doesn't count on the danger surrounding her target…or her irresistible attraction to him.

#1158 HIS BEST FRIEND'S BABY by Mallory Kane
Black Hills Brotherhood
When his best friend's baby is kidnapped, the rugged survival expert is on call to help rescue her child. As they follow the kidnapper's trail up a remote mountain, they must battle the elements and an undeniable passion.

#1159 PEEK-A-BOO PROTECTOR by Rita Herron
Seeing Double
The sheriff admires the work of the child advocate, but her latest charge, an abandoned baby, is the target of merciless kidnappers. Her life is on the line, and he's discovering that protecting her may be more than just a job….

#1160 COVERT COOTCHIE-COOTCHIE-COO
by Ann Voss Peterson
Seeing Double
Someone wants to harm the baby boy left aboard his ship, and the captain hires a tenacious P.I. to get some answers. As they work together to keep the child safe, startling truths are not the only things they uncover….

www.eHarlequin.com

HICNMBPA0809